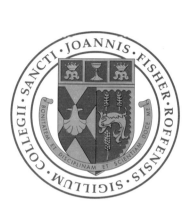

BLOOD GOLD

BLOOD GOLD

MICHAEL CADNUM

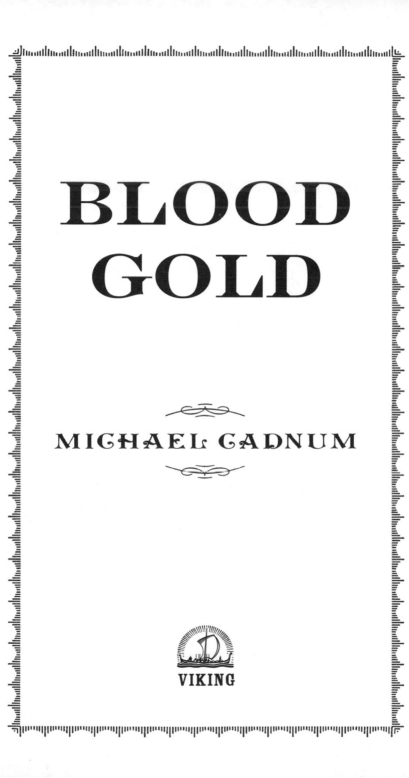

VIKING

VIKING
Published by Penguin Group
Penguin Young Readers Group, 345 Hudson Street, New York, New York 10014, U.S.A.
Penguin Books Ltd, 80 Strand, London WC2R 0RL, England
Penguin Books Australia Ltd, 250 Camberwell Road, Camberwell, Victoria 3124, Australia
Penguin Books Canada Ltd, 10 Alcorn Avenue, Toronto, Ontario, Canada M4V 3B2
Penguin Books (N.Z.) Ltd, 182-190 Wairau Road, Auckland 10, New Zealand

Published in 2004 by Viking, a division of Penguin Young Readers Group

1 3 5 7 9 10 8 6 4 2

LIBRARY OF CONGRESS CATALOGING-IN-PUBLICATION DATA
Cadnum, Michael.
Blood gold / by Michael Cadnum.
p. cm.
Summary: After an arduous journey, Will Dwinelle and his friend Ben finally reach
California in 1849 intending to bring home the man who betrayed the honor of a girl back
home in Philadelphia, but find themselves tempted by the riches of the Gold Rush.
ISBN 0-670-05884-X (hardcover)
[1. Gold mines and mining—California—History—19th century. 2. Conduct of life—Fiction.
3. Voyages and travels—Fiction. 4. Adventure and adventurers—Fiction.
5. San Francisco (Calif.)—History—19th century—Fiction.] I. Title.
PZ7.C11724Bl 2004
[Fic]—dc22
2003022362

Printed in U.S.A.
Set in Granjon
Book design by Kelley McIntyre

⊰[BLOOD GOLD]⊱

PART ONE
LUST

·⊲[CHAPTER 1]⊳·

Rain fell through the jungle.

And then, with a pulse of lightning, it began to come down all the harder, great sheets of water.

My hat was soaked through in an instant, the mid-afternoon shadowy sunlight swallowed by cloud. Ben Pomeroy, my friend and traveling companion, patted his pack mule, water splashing from the animal's hide. The beast stood with its ears bent forward to keep the downpour out of them. Ben looked back at me through the deluge with a smile, gave me a theatrical wave, and laughed at the madness of it all.

Weary as I was, I had to laugh, too.

The trail guides had told us we were one day east of Panama City, on our trek through ooze and slime, mules and men standing slack-jointed under the weight of the falling water. All of us were on our way to the goldfields of California, taking the less usual jungle route through the Isthmus of Panama instead of the land route across North America. We had endured an ocean voyage down the East Coast from Philadelphia and New York into increasingly thick, warm weather, and now we faced this cataract.

It was already November in the gold-fevered year of 1849, and we were making slow progress, up to our boot tops in tropical muck, with a long line of fellow gold seekers in single file along the muddy trail. The colonel—responsible for our safety during the jungle leg of our trip—had warned us to stay on the path.

Ben put his hand to his ear and pointed, signaling that he heard something of interest in the jungle. He called out something, too, but I couldn't hear. He motioned me to follow, but I shook my head.

"If you get lost in there—" I called, my voice faint in the rain. *I'm not coming in after you,* I did not bother to add.

But I knew I would.

Outlandish creatures had been creeping out of the underbrush all afternoon. I had crushed a centipede by accident, squashing it with my boot, and Aaron Sweetland, hurrying into the underbrush with another bout of diarrhea, had stepped on an iguana the size of a dog. The iguana had been uninjured, by all reports, but Aaron's temper was not improved. Howler monkeys thronged the broad-leafed trees. Colonel Legrand had shot one that morning, and stretched him out beside the trail.

Now it was late in the day and I hadn't eaten anything but a mouthful of jerked beef for breakfast a thousand years ago.

I called after my friend, but there was no further sign of him. I was worried, although the other men on the trail gave no sign of concern.

"Ben, come back here," I cried out as loudly as I could, my words drowned by the rain.

I reached for the Bowie knife in my belt, loosening it in its scabbard. It would be ready if I had to rush in after Ben and save his life.

I called again, but there was no answer.

Dr. Merrill came back down the line of pack mules, rain dancing off the brim of his hat. "Is he ill?" asked the doctor.

"No, he's just—" *He's simply being himself*, I would have added.

"I wouldn't leave the trail, unless there was an emergency," said the youthful doctor, concern in his voice.

I was uneasy, wondering what was taking Ben so long. Maybe he had been taken ill with malaria, yellow jack, or some jungle fever I dared not name.

Too long.

Ben was taking too long.

I had no choice—I slipped into the undergrowth after him.

···❧ CHAPTER 2 ❧···

Leaves spouted water down my neck, tree roots and generations of rotted plant life slippery under my boots. I had to hang on to twigs and glossy leaves to keep from stumbling, every glossy, broad green span of vegetation spouting water.

Ben struggled, his boot trapped between two sinuous roots.

I tried to wrestle his leg free, but his ankle was wedged hard, and the tree overhead gave a subtle, deep-throated groan. All day we had been stumbling over huge tropical behemoths, trees that had fallen across the trail. It took no great imagination to see that in a few heartbeats Ben could be crushed.

"I heard a parrot calling," he said.

"Did you?" I said, in a tone of exasperation, realizing that even if I slit his boot he would still be trapped—

his foot had plunged all the way into the subsoil.

"I just had to take a look," he added apologetically.

A pair of wings burst upward, the bird shrilling wordlessly as he flew, flapping off through the rain. He was joined by a flock, an insane choir of birds, looking wet and brilliant, a ceaseless, cackling jubilation that brought a certain happiness to my heart.

The tree overhead gave another threatening groan.

"Willie," said Ben, continuing his shaky explanation, "that bird is just like Reverend Josselyn's."

I answer to William, Willie, or Will. I am named after my father's older brother, the same William Washington Dwinelle who was killed while rescuing passengers on the steamboat *Algonquin,* in the winter of 1830. My parents had both died of typhoid, and I was being raised on the stew-and-dumpling fare provided by my mother's younger sister, my aunt Jane. I missed my parents badly, but with every passing season they were becoming more like legendary people who had lived in a bygone era, while each day thrust me forward into new prospects.

I didn't like to think of home just then—it seemed so far away. Reverend Josselyn's bird could yell *Isaiah*, the reverend's Christian name, the only word he knew, and give off a strange, very human chuckle. I missed the bird, the way it would take a piece of toast out of a visitor's hand, and I wished I was there right now in the parlor with the clergyman and his daughter Elizabeth.

"Very much," I agreed.

7

I had my knife in my hand, and sawed at the great green roots.

I liked Ben, but sometimes I wished he wasn't so impulsive, always hurrying off to look at some amazing sight. We made our way back to the trail, Ben walking with a slight limp, and I hated the sound that rushed after us through the undergrowth, the tree collapsing, bird and animal life fleeing into the recesses of the jungle scrub.

All the mules in the long line of pack animals had come to a stop, the men hunched over waiting for a signal to come down from ahead telling us what we were going to do. We had been afraid of bandits all that day—ever since a traveler heading east, one of the few individuals traveling that direction, had reported men armed with shotguns in the jungle, waiting for a mule train rich enough to be worth the trouble.

No one besides Ben made a move to walk off into the foliage—except to answer a call of nature. A special case was poor Aaron Sweetland, who had the flux, and a fever that made him weak. Every one of us had a fondness for Aaron, who had the only decent singing voice among us. Dr. Merrill had given him salts, and Richardson's Bitters, and even had him chewing charcoal by the spoonful, but no medicine worked. Even now Aaron was struggling off into the jungle yet again, unbuttoning his trousers.

The natives of the Isthmus of Panama carried machetes, long tools much the same as the cutlass, and rumor had rippled up and down the line of travelers that two

Virginians had been found dead with their throats cut, half eaten by ants beside the Chagres River. It was true that the Spanish-speaking people I had met in Chagres town, and all along the trail, had been gracious and businesslike, but stories were told of violent jungle dwellers who hated fortune-seeking Yankees.

Ben had read a book about the jungles back in Pennsylvania before we left many weeks before. He had reported that the isthmus was only three days' travel across, and much of it by river, but the land route that completed the journey west was "through a territory marked by the jaguar, a flesh-eating cat, and the anaconda, one of nature's largest and most powerful serpents."

Now Colonel Legrand came back down the line, giving out plugs of chewing tobacco to the men who wanted it. He tugged a leather strap now and then to keep luggage secure on the backs of the mules.

Legrand was our trail guide, his services provided as a part of the price of our ticket with the steamship company, and he was the only man among us with any fighting experience, having been a part of Zachary Taylor's army invading Mexico in 1846. It was said that he had killed an officer of the Mexican army with a bayonet thrust, and he looked like a man who could have done it—sweating, sunburned, his cheek fat with a plug of molasses-cured tobacco.

"Are you men all right?" asked the colonel, looking me in the eye.

I nodded, my hat heavy with water. The rain had slowed down. I took a cut of the black, sweet-flavored leaf the colonel offered me with thanks, and when I had it tucked securely in my cheek, I asked, "We're going to bed down here?"

I tried to sound manly and indifferent to where I spread my blanket, but in my eighteen years on earth I had not imagined such a hot, wet, inhuman place.

"I don't think anyone mentioned beds," said Colonel Legrand, with a laugh. He wasn't a real colonel, I suspect—people just called him that out of respect. "Neither one of you," he added, "would be reckless enough to wander off into the underbrush, would you?"

"No, sir," answered Ben. He favored his right leg—the one that had been trapped—keeping his weight off it.

The trail guide called out *hey-up*, and the mules stirred, plodding forward. Their hooves were unshod for service on this jungle track; they could pick their way through roots and mud much better than humans.

And for an instant the romance of all this swept me, and I was happy. Ben was of the opinion that I am too changeable, but surely there are worse traits. With the remnants of rain echoing like applause off the broad leaves, and the smell of spice in the air, I spat tobacco juice and was about to feel pretty sure of myself again. I wondered if maybe Ben and I could get accustomed to exploring unknown regions of the earth, and other such adventures, after we had found the scoundrel we were hunting in California.

We passed a snake hanging from the crook of a tree, headless but still writhing.

When we got to the wide place in the trail, night had nearly fallen. The jungle heat teased us with hungry mosquitoes and a ceaseless chirping Ben had said were tree frogs.

"We need volunteers for first watch," said Colonel Legrand. He held up a musket with a bayonet attached to it to indicate the responsibilities involved.

I wasn't feeling particularly brave, but buoyed by my cheerful mood. Besides, I just didn't want to lie down on the ground right then, not where spiders and serpents made their homes.

"I don't mind if I stand the first watch," I volunteered.

I knew I might as well get accustomed to putting up with hardship. After all, I was not going to California to seek pay dirt, like all the rest of these hopeful, ambitious travelers. Ben and I had a special purpose for wandering so far from home.

We were looking for a particular individual in the gold country, and we fully intended to find him.

·≼ CHAPTER 3 ≽·

Colonel Legrand sized me up with a smile, perhaps thinking I was too young and green to be trusted with a musket.

I am tall and broad-shouldered, and unafraid of any kind of hard work. Mr. Donald Ansted, my employer back home, and author of the pamphlet *Some Remarks on the Prospects of Repeating Firearms,* had been an expert gunsmith, when the carriage-repairing business was slow. He had always praised my willingness to put in extra hours repairing weapons.

I knew enough to say, "The gunpowder's so wet it wouldn't spark anyway, Colonel."

I had test-fired a few guns with Mr. Ansted, and I knew that at twenty paces you had a better chance of hitting a man with a frying pan than a musket ball.

Colonel Legrand gave a laugh and put the musket

into my hands. The weapon was heavy, and gave off the scent of gun oil.

"It'll shoot," said the colonel simply. He meant: be careful.

Ben hoped someday to study Shakespeare at a university, but I had more lowly ambitions. I had dreams of redesigning carriages, or repairing the fowling pieces of clergymen and scholars. Reverend Spinks was the master of the Methodist School of Classics and the Arts I had attended; Ben had studied at Professor and Mrs. Holliday's Boys' School. Ben and I had been friends and neighbors since childhood, and we both enjoyed the same stories of King Arthur and Richard Lionheart. I was not destined to be a gentleman, however. A skilled craft, working with my hands, would be enough for me.

The other guard the colonel posted that night was Isom Gill, a man who had been seasick every day on the side-wheeler out of New York. A cabinetmaker by trade, he was, like me, neither lofty gentleman nor unlettered day laborer. He was one of the few among us to have a really decent gun, a double-barreled English firearm with one barrel rifled, the other smoothbore.

Ben said he would stand watch with me, but I told him to get some rest. Mr. Gill had a determined set to his mouth, eager to prove himself, and I believed we would be in good hands. A few of us had packed guns or pistols when we left our families and homes, but all day we had been passing cast-off fowling pieces and flintlock pistols, already rusting in the vegetation, along with piles of heavy wool clothing. Dr. Merrill kept a Navy Colt revolver in a mahogany case, the sole example of the newly invented repeating pistol I had ever seen.

The doctor bent down over Aaron Sweetland, asked a question, and straightened, heading back to his trunk for a blue bottle of laudanum, the one sure medicine for cramps. He administered the potion to his shivering, sweating patient. We had buried a blacksmith at the trail-head by the river, and a jolly gray-haired cooper named O. P. Schuster, and Dr. Merrill had confided to me that he suspected there would be more outbreaks of fever.

The doctor met my eye as he stepped back to his medical bag, pressing the stopper back into the bottle. "Mr. Dwinelle, every bandit in Central America would faint dead away at the sight of you."

I laughed. It was true that I was tall enough, and sturdily built enough to fancy myself a man among men. But inside I knew I was a rank novice at adventure, and just for now I was happy to keep dramatic thrills in the distant future.

The musket the colonel thrust into my hands was an old Brown Bess–type weapon, the sort the British army had used for generations, the barrel well oiled but the lock tarnished from the damp. I imagine I made a tough-looking figure, in my slouch hat and heavy trousers, a foot-long knife in my belt. In fact, any one of my traveling companions would have frightened off the toughest alley fighter in New York or Philadelphia. A more dirty-looking set of men I had never seen.

Many other traveling companies were camped in the same clearing, and it was some time before tents had been arranged in spots that were not knee-deep in water. After Ben brought me a plate of fried salt beef and a cup of thick, sweet coffee, I felt about ready to fight off an army of robbers.

Later I would marvel at my confidence that all would be well.

The night was pure darkness, and the smoke from our fire lifted straight up. I tried to find a place where the smoke drifted down again, weighed down by the humidity. When I did, I stood there surrounded by wood smoke, even though my eyes smarted—the smoke discouraged the needling attacks of the mosquitoes.

I must have had what my late father used to call "a special inkling" what was going to happen that night, because I kept well away from Mr. Gill and his expensive gun. When he came around the camp full of sleeping men, his footsteps shuffling the sodden underbrush, I circled away from him, even though it meant that the blood-starved insects could find me again. They stung hard and often, with tiny, keening voices.

I heard the distant, distinctive double-click not long afterward. Even at this distance, through the thick air and the sound of snoring, there was no mistaking the sound, the double hammers of Gill's Bond Street gun being cocked.

I wanted to call out, *What is it?*

It would be just like a gang of bandits to rush us while nearly all of us were stretched out on the ground like this.

Before I could make a sound both barrels fired.

The thud of the smoothbore and the crack of the rifled barrel sounded like the reports of two entirely different weapons. The rush of wings and startled bird cries echoed off through the dark jungle, animals frightened by the noise.

Humans stirred; frightened voices joined with the snorts of startled mules.

Colonel Legrand called out, "Mr. Gill, what's wrong?"

There was no answer.

·⋈{ CHAPTER 4 }⋈·

I rushed through the dark, not bothering to cock my gun, knowing that with the darkness, the hubbub of voices, and the venerable age of my weapon, I would have better luck with the cold steel of the bayonet.

"Mr. Gill, what do you see?" Colonel Legrand was demanding, lanterns sputtering to life. The colonel hurried through the camp carrying a coiled whip.

He called for everyone to stand back and calm down. People did just what he said, fading back toward the ebbing campfire, falling quiet.

Dr. Merrill was huddled over someone at the jungle's edge in quaking lantern light, the lamps held high by apprehensive, unsteady hands.

Aaron Sweetland sprawled, gasping for breath, blood bubbling. In the shivering pool of light his head gleamed, half scarlet, and gore welled from his shirtfront.

Men turned angrily, seizing Mr. Gill, the expensive gun snatched away and passed high, hand to hand, until the colonel took it.

"Whip him!" said several voices, the loudest of them David Cowden, an office clerk from Williamsport.

"Put him in irons!" said Albert Kerr, a former neighbor of Mr. Gill's. Heavy fists began to fall on Mr. Gill in the surging light of the campfire, where wet wood was dumped on the embers, raising a flume of illuminated smoke.

I pushed my way through the crowd of sweaty, angry men, and stood before Mr. Gill, the musket level in my hands.

Firelight gleamed along the bayonet, and men fell silent at the sight.

"It was an accident," I said.

"If he dies, it's murder," rasped Mr. Kerr, a lens grinder by trade. He wore oval, silver-rimmed spectacles, the lenses glittering in the lamplight.

"Manslaughter," corrected Mr. Cowden, a dimpled, soft-looking man who had once studied law. Soon the anger was spent in a bickering debate over which legal term would apply. But there was relief in the men's voices, seizing upon legal argument instead of further punishing Mr. Gill, who was on his knees.

"Thank you, Willie!" said Mr. Gill, clutching at my trouser leg.

I felt an instant of revulsion at his gratitude, and wanted to step well away from him, to separate from his grasp. It wasn't that I particularly disliked the man—I didn't want any of his bad luck.

But then Colonel Legrand said, "Well done, Dwinelle," and clapped me on the arm. He helped Mr. Gill to his feet, and half forced him through the already dissipating tangle of men.

"The sentry mistook an intruder," called out the colonel, and the military character of his voice settled all of us further, giving a soldier's dignity to the mishap.

But Aaron Sweetland was bleeding hard.

ᐧᒃ CHAPTER 5 ᑫᐧ

D r. Merrill stood at the fire, stirring the smoking coals with a ramrod.

Aaron Sweetland had been heavily dosed with medicine from the blue bottle and he was no longer sobbing with pain. One ear had been shot away, and the rifle shot had drilled him right through his shoulder, just below the collarbone.

Morning was not far away; the camp cook was carrying a kettle through the dark.

Dr. Merrill turned from the fire, bleary-eyed from the smoke, with the tip of the rod glowing red.

"If you have the heart for it, William," said the doctor, "I can use your help."

Stomach for it, he should have said. I knew all about cauterizing wounds—Aunt Jane and my sister and I had lived upstairs from a surgeon who treated barge-men and their knife wounds.

I knew too well what was going to happen. But I have an optimistic outlook on things that often causes me to utter outright untruths. "I'm happy to help," I heard this cheerful part of me sing out.

Ben took a deep breath and shook his head.

Dr. Merrill was only a few years older than us, but with his wooden box of drugs and clean-shaven countenance he was like another sort of man altogether. Furthermore, he reminded both of us of home, where kind-voiced men and women exchanged pleasantries. I treasured the memory of Philadephia's Walnut Street, where whale-oil lamps cast a silver glow over Elizabeth, the reverend's daughter, as she read to me from *Macbeth*.

Ben and I had been happy to help Dr. Merrill at small tasks on board the ship, holding a pan while he bled a sailor, repacking his books when a storm swell sent them all over the deck. But cauterizing wounds was one of the most painful procedures medicine required. A hot iron was understood to seal the wound and encourage heal-ing, but by all accounts it was painful beyond belief.

Now Dr. Merrill was thrusting the ramrod back into the coals one last time and asking Colonel Legrand, "Would you have some brandy for all of us just before we begin?"

"All we have is the local rum, Dr. Merrill," said the colonel sympathetically. "I haven't seen brandy since Christmas."

I tilted the heavy bottle, and found that the liquor tasted of molasses, hot peppers, and poison. I could barely swallow. I passed the bottle on to Ben. He took a long drink and coughed, just like me.

Dr. Merrill took a drink from the bottle, too, and swallowed it down like water. Then he withdrew the glowing tip of the ramrod from the fire.

He strode purposefully over to the place where Mr. Sweetland had been carried by his friends, men from his hometown who had formed the Tioga County Mining and Assaying Company. Many small groups had set up such companies, signing bylaws and solemn promises to help each other. If nothing else, it provided support for times like this, and, if the worst happened, companions who would arrange decent burial.

"Hold the lamp high, Ben," said Dr. Merrill, his voice firm. "Willie, you hold Mr. Sweetland down."

Mr. Sweetland was agape, blessedly half-stunned by the opium-and-spirits he had been swallowing.

The glowing iron approached the wound in his shoulder.

I couldn't help thinking that this was the sort of injury I would give Ezra Nevin—when I found him. If he so much as gave me the least argument about coming home with me.

If he gave me the least quibble about the harm and embarrassment he'd created for Elizabeth.

·⊰[CHAPTER 6]⊱·

Wherever he went, everyone liked Ezra.

I liked him, too—despite my loyalty to Elizabeth. Anyone would. He had a smile nearly as infectious as Ben's, and a manly, rough elegance that made dogs fawn and grown men clap him on the back.

The younger son of the family that published the Philadelphia *North American,* he had traveled to London and Paris, spending a year on the sort of Grand Tour most young men can only dream about. He could speak French, play the piano, and had recently met a man on the field of honor, prepared to fight a duel.

Ezra had brought the brace of horse pistols—the very dueling weapons themselves—for my employer to repair shortly afterward. They were silver-chased .65 caliber flintlocks, made by Hadley of London. A morning rain shower had dampened them, and Ezra had wanted them cleaned and oiled by an expert.

"I hope I never set eyes on Murray again, Willie," he had said with a shaky laugh. "He ran away before I could take a shot at him, and that's the worst sort of enemy to have."

"One that can run away?" I said, jokingly.

"No," said Ezra in all seriousness. "A proud man who's embarrassed himself."

I knew Murray about as well as I knew Ezra. Where Ezra was quick with a smile, and easy to admire, Murray was a young man I almost felt sorry for—he was so difficult to like. Ezra's newspaper had criticized the Murray banking family as heavy investors in the "rat-thick hovels for the poor" in an article I suspect Ezra had penned himself.

The two young men had met in Rittenhouse Square, exchanged unpleasantries, and the duel had been inevitable given the high-minded energy of Ezra and the stolid pride of Samuel Murray. The big redhead was an anxious man, with a broad pale forehead and a humorless laugh. He had a way of cracking his knuckles and toying with his watch fob as he complained that the harness I mended, or the wheel I repaired, was too late, overpriced, and the workmanship unsatisfactory.

At the same time, Murray was not a person you'd want as an enemy—rumor told of his favorite sport, shooting stray dogs with a fowling piece. Rumor filled in the details of Murray's disappearance after the abortive duel. Some said he was having a repeating pistol custom-designed in London. Others suggested that he'd fled to Boston, where he was looking for sterner, more violent companions, so he could return to Philadelphia and shoot Ezra like a cur.

Ezra's family newspaper had carried dispatches from San Francisco on its front page the year before, a California official crowing "your streams have minnows, ours are choked with gold." Ezra found a graceful and perfectly respectable reason to leave town with one of his card-playing companions, a good-natured gentleman named Andrew Follette. They were by no means the first men in Philadelphia to head west, but they were the first I had known personally.

Ezra waved to Ben and me as servants packed his brand-new, bright-hinged trunk into a wagon, calling out the well-worn "Ho! For California!"—laughing as he spoke. It was his laugh you'd always remember about him, his white teeth flashing, a sunny, stirring sound that made you join in, despite yourself.

Only in his fresh absence did Elizabeth write me a letter, her beautiful, usually carefully quilled handwriting unsteady with feeling. We arranged a secret meeting, late at night, the neighborhood asleep, out by the green where during happier times the summer horse races were held.

There in the dark she confessed to me that Ezra had sworn to marry her, and had taken advantage of her passion for him. She whispered a further confession, halting, barely able to put it into words. She believed that she was carrying Ezra's child.

Perhaps I had read too many tales of chivalrous heroes. Perhaps I was hostage to feelings toward Elizabeth I had not fully realized until then. But I stood there under the stars and swore on the graves of my parents, with God as my witness, that I would find Ezra Nevin, and bring him back.

The next morning Ben had chuckled in amazement. "So old Ezra is a scamp, as well as a gentleman."

"I guess the two are not contradictory," I said.

Ben never hesitated.

We unearthed our hard-saved money and left heartfelt, loving notes for our families. It was a simple matter, in my case, with both my parents dead of fever, and Aunt Jane worn with the trouble of cooking my meals. Ben's family had two older sons, already happily busy in the family drayage business. Perhaps the Pomeroys had hoped, without saying so in words, that Ben might leave for the West, and come back to them with chests of placer gold.

We departed on the Express Line from the Walnut Street wharf. We ferried across the Delaware River, took the railway to South Amboy, New Jersey, and rode a steamboat to New York. It cost three dollars each, the trip lasting just under five hours.

Now Aaron's sobs were subsiding, and the early-morning sun was just beginning to weaken the darkness, bird life stirring all around us.

The injured man was carried tenderly to a wagon in the early light. Two other men lay down with him—they had been overcome by fever in the night. Anxious rumors had swept through the gold seekers, of a mysterious fever that was swallowing men in the prime of life. There was a hospital in Panama City, we were told, run by a German physician named Hauser and his daughter. The more optimistic among us enjoyed the first morning chew of tobacco and agreed that no doubt Dr. Hauser would have a tonic that would break every fever.

"I bet it's not as bad as we imagine," I heard my own voice say, as though I knew anything about it.

"I bet you're right," several voices agreed. Folks chewing tobacco often appear ruminative and wise. You chew, shift your quid, lean forward and spit, and feel like a philosopher. We had ourselves convinced we were in no danger at all.

The truth was, we were terrified to think that this disease might catch up with us. No man dared to whisper the three-syllable curse.

Cholera.

There was no known defense against it, and no cure. Whole villages succumbed to it, all around the world, and ships arrived in port, their crews devastated.

I said a special prayer for the shot man, and for the others, too.

Including Ben and me.

·≼ CHAPTER 7 ≽·

Flocks of raucous parrots broke from the trees overhead as we made our way along the trail. Dr. Merrill rode beside his patient, putting out a steadying arm when Aaron Sweetland tried to sit up in the back of the wagon.

Isom Gill walked alongside, offering encouragement. "We're all coming back rich, Aaron," he said.

It was proper for Isom Gill to show concern for Aaron, and the company was more forgiving now. Men began to share anecdotes from back home, accidents with firearms and farming equipment that had proven less than fatal.

The medication gave Aaron the spirit to sing in a weak voice, a pretty hymn about walking with Jesus.

The jungle began to grow sparse, and we began to pass the simple cane-hut buildings of farmers and the broad thick fields of sugarcane. Children playing in sandy streams watched us as we passed, their mothers and older sisters protected from the sun by white shawls.

The adults, loading bunches of bananas into oxcarts, driving scrawny mules, did little to acknowledge our passage, but I waved to a little boy as naked as a toothpick, and he pointed at us and uttered something in Spanish. A pretty dark-eyed woman, in a sweeping, blue-fringed mantle, came forward to take the little boy's hand, no doubt thinking we were marauders, and a sure threat to the countryside.

I shifted the tobacco in my mouth and tipped my hat, and the woman lowered her eyes and gave the gentlest of smiles. One glance back at Ben, to see if he had observed this civility, made me realize once again how rough we all looked. My friend, who could name the great scientists of history, from Aristotle to Newton, looked like the lowest sort of character, his features shadowed by his broad hat, his youthful chin in need of a razor.

But he stopped to speak to the woman in the blue mantle, tipping his hat and wishing her a good day.

She studied him with a sidelong glance, in no hurry to respond at once, but in no hurry to depart, either.

Ben added, "We're *cabelleros*, bound for California."

The young woman broke into a smile at this, and said something in return, a half-mocking, half-welcoming statement in Spanish.

Not to be outdone, Ben tried out a little more

Spanish of his own, something he must have worked up from the phrase book I had seen him studying on board the ship.

He uttered an entire sentence in the language, and she was talking right back.

The mules and jungle-weary travelers plodded past us on the trail. "Are you coming along, Ben," I said with a degree of exasperation, "or are you going to talk this woman to death?"

We had walked on a good distance before Ben remarked, "Willie, I believe that young senorita took a sort of passing liking to me."

"If there wasn't a real woman around," I said, "you'd talk to a statue, or a picture on a wall."

"Is it possible," queried Ben with his usual good humor, "that you envy me my charms?"

I would not have used such lofty phrasing. It was true, however, that I was more than a little jealous of my friend's way with womenfolk.

"Not at all," I lied.

"Not even a little?" Ben asked.

I am agreeable enough to look at, I have been told, with russet hair and eyes the color of well water. But when I gaze into a mirror I see someone staring right back, unsure of his own worth. A powerful shyness makes me feel speechless around some ladies. Elizabeth was the only young woman I'd ever known who took the trouble to confide in me. I could close my eyes and see her face.

Aaron Sweetland sat up as we came within the out-lying district of Panama City. The early-afternoon sun glowed on red-tiled roofs, and vines climbed tall, crumbling walls. Cows lowed, goats skittered, and scrawny mules traversed narrow cobbled streets.

"By God, fellows," said Aaron Sweetland, his voice weak but joyful, "I believe we're near Panama City!"

·◄[CHAPTER 8]►·

The town's jungle approach was defended by an ancient wall. A rusting cannon gaped out over the jungle vista, shrouded by bright green vines.

Dwelling shacks and booths selling food sprawled toward the outlying fields, well beyond the decaying fortifications. Parrots on perches called out greetings in Spanish as we approached, and shopkeepers held up tall displays festooned with samples of their wares, everything from soap to shoes. Church bells echoed all around.

A sweet smell thickened the air, tobacco leaf and molasses, with an undercurrent of manure. The scent of burning sugarcane drifted across the plazas. Bins displayed gleaming mounds of citrus fruits, lemons and small, perfectly round oranges. Iron-studded doors and rust-grilled windows protected some of the stately buildings from our curious eyes. Stalls were decorated with fluttering, bright ribbons, sausages and bright bottles of colored liquors. Nearly every citizen we beheld was smoking tobacco, the lace-shawled ladies holding small, dark cigars, the men drawing on cheroots.

Colonel Legrand announced that our trunks and equipment would be taken to the Uncle Sam Hotel.

I was sorry to take leave of the old soldier, and I said so.

"You'll forget all about me and this pitiful jungle," he said with a laugh. "You're off to see the elephant."

That was the way people referred to the California adventure. Newspapers would recount that a newly formed company was "Off to See the Elephant," and the few just returned from San Francisco would hang "I've Seen the Elephant!" from a window. Whether you found riches or not, no one wanted to miss out on the world-shaking experience of the rush for the precious metal.

The Tioga Company paused at the three-story building with black balconies that, judging by the flag hanging unmoving in the hot humid noon, served as the American consulate. Coins were counted out, and Dr. Merrill pocketed them, thanking Aaron Sweetland's companions, and then Aaron began to complain as his associates tried to help him up the steps to the consulate.

"You're not going to ship me home!" he cried.

No one could respond to that, as if the entire company

had been discovered committing a crime of deception.

Then friendly voices reasoned with him, one man saying that there was no shame in arranging passage back to New York because of two grievous wounds, either one of which would have slain a buffalo.

"Dr. Merrill," cried Aaron Sweetland, "tell them I'm fit to sail for California."

Our medical friend put a thoughtful finger to his lips, and, for the moment, made no further remark.

Mr. Sweetland bellowed, with surprising strength for a stricken man, "Mr. Gill, I want you to help me."

"Of course I will," said Mr. Gill, stepping forward, hat in hand. "If the company will allow me, I'll do everything in my power to see you all the way to the goldfields."

I had never heard a statement put so well.

"That won't be necessary," said one of the Tioga Company, but not unkindly.

"There is, I think most of you will agree," said Dr. Merrill, "a certain justice to Mr. Gill's offer."

The Tioga Company ultimately accepted the doctor's view. Doctors, like clergymen, were an upright authority.

Dr. Merrill reminded the two of us that we could by no means be certain that the ship would be waiting for us, so we scurried through the streets, along with many of our companions, anxiously hoping our plans would remain intact.

The afternoon was hot, but a sea breeze stirred the

leaves of the palm trees shading the fountains. Everywhere the eye fell some parasitic vine was overgrowing a wall or monument. Even the tallest Moorish tower was succumbing to the insidious claws of creeping, flowering plants. The town had been stirring on our arrival, but the sultry plazas were nearly empty now. The only men on the street now were Americans, spitting and smoking, hurrying through the bright afternoon sun.

The harbor was grander than I had expected, with long stone breakwaters and sailing ships, most of them three-masted barks, rigging hanging empty and slack in the heavy sun. I wished Elizabeth had been there to see the deep, beautiful blue of the water. A sign at the dock announced the fact that the Pacific Mail steamship *California* would depart at nine o'clock the following morning.

We were hungry, and thirsty, too, but we had to be certain. To our relief, the steamship herself was actually moored at the wharf.

A ship of greater character would be hard to imagine. She had three masts, with tightly furled sails, but her power was expected to be supplied by the steam-driven wheel along her side. The first steamship to enter San Francisco Bay, the *California* had begun plying the western waters only eight months earlier, but there were continual problems that delayed travelers. Her crew had deserted for three months during early summer, everyone but the cook and the captain heading off to join the stampede for fortune.

There were many other ships that ferried gold seekers, but this one was the most famous. Crates of provisions, wooden boxes stained with seepage, were being hoisted into her interior. We all walked reverently up and down the wharf in the ship's shadow, and Ben said she was the finest ship he had ever seen.

A seaman suspended in a sling touched black paint on scars along the ship's railing, the result, Dr. Merrill suggested, of a minor collision with another vessel. The ship's man looked at us and paused, his paintbrush in his hand. I waved, and the mariner gave a salute with his brush.

I approached a ticket agent leaning on the counter of a whitewashed wooden booth. He was smoking a short black clay pipe, and reading a worn, leather-bound Bible. A nameplate at his elbow gave his name, T. T. Rowe. I asked if there was any record of my good friend Ezra Nevin passing through this port.

"Son, how on earth would I tell this individual," inquired Mr. Rowe, slowly raising his eyes from the scriptures, "from every other eager traveler?"

···⊰{ CHAPTER 9 }⊱···

He shook his head after I had described Ezra, down to his silver belt buckle.

He gave me a sympathetic smile, keeping a forefinger on the page he was reading—Proverbs 10—and speaking around the stem of his pipe, he said, "You'll catch up with your friend, son—don't worry."

"I wonder if I will," I said doubtfully.

"We ship great bags of mail to San Francisco," said the ticket agent. "Bags filled to bursting with letters from home, addressed to 'Johnny So-and-So, along the Sacramento or the Yuba Rivers,' or 'Jacob Howdy, Somewhere in the Goldfields.'" He concluded rhetorically, "And do you know what happens to these precious letters?"

"Tell us," I must have said. Or perhaps my manner spoke for me.

"It might take weeks, but most of the letters find

their due recipient." He leaned forward, and each word was emphasized by a feather of smoke from the bowl of his pipe. "You could die up there in the Sierra," he said, like a man delivering good news. "But you most assuredly won't get lost."

"If you would let us take a look at your list of passengers," Ben suggested, "we'd be grateful."

I offered Mr. Rowe the remains of a twist of chewing tobacco, a parting gift from Colonel Legrand. He accepted it, took the pipe from his mouth, and stuffed the entire wad into his mouth. He took his time placing the chew squarely in his cheek. Then he took a large book, wide and scored with faint blue lines, and set it on the counter before him.

They were all there, written in a fine clerk's hand, rows of names penned in brown ink. It did not take him long to put a finger on *E. Nevin*. "Ah, that spirited young fellow," said Mr. Rowe. "He gave me a dollar for arranging help with his trunk."

He thought for a while, working the tobacco quid around in his cheek. He spat into the brass urn at his feet, a wide-mouthed spittoon soiled with expectoration and cigar ash. "Unless I'm mistaken, I do believe some other man was asking after this very gentleman," he said. "Not long afterward. A big man, with a couple of hard-looking companions."

Ben tugged at my arm, with an apologetic pat of his stomach.

I knew how he felt—I had never felt so famished

in my life. And I gave no further thought to the ticket agent's news, I was so distracted by my hunger.

A handsome building across the square, shaded by trees, its confines protected by tall, moss-darkened walls, was surmounted by a tall limestone statue I took to be an image of Jesus' mother. Nuns came and went from the iron-worked front door of this convent, and I felt the beautiful strangeness of the place, with the scent of flowers, spices, and verdure in the air, settle in on me.

The doctor stopped by a nearby hotel that served as a hospital, a graceful building with a cloak of flowering vines along one wall. While Dr. Merrill checked on the disposition of his two fever-wracked patients, Ben and I sat beside a fountain that played water gently over its mossy interior.

The town sported a number of large black birds, elegant in flight, and as we admired the sight of them, a whiskery man in stained canvas trousers made his way unsteadily toward us.

"You're too late!" he said.

I could smell the rum at three paces.

"If you're not there in California already," he continued, "you might as well turn around and slog your way home."

"Are they running out of gold?" asked Ben.

And I felt an inner current of anxiety, too. *All the gleaming treasure would be gone.*

"No," said the stranger, his red beard tangled, his

shirtfront missing buttons. "They brought out nuggets as big as your fist, and men are still getting rich."

I was surprised at how relieved I felt at this news.

The first trace of the valuable California lode had been found in January 1848. In December of that year, the newspapers had trumpeted President Polk's announcement that the gold was real, that it was plentiful, and that, in effect, it was there for the taking. American money was nearly always in the form of gold or silver coin. Banknotes, issued by local institutions, were less popular, and few businesspeople liked accepting notes from a distant city. There was no national paper money, and this meant that the precious metal being shoveled from the Sierra foothills was pure, instantaneous wealth.

"But the only people really raking in the riches," continued the drunken American, "are the men selling spirits, and the whores."

Dr. Merrill came toward us across the plaza, walking in his quick, distinctive way, his medical bag in his hand.

"And doctors!" said the unsteady American. "Doctors and gamblers will fill their pockets with the stuff."

The stranger looked away with a sigh. Then he turned back, fixing first Ben and then me with his bloodshot eye, including the doctor with a final, particularly urgent glance. Dr. Merrill seemed to grow even leaner and more quiet under this examination. "Surely I've done you no offense," said Dr. Merrill quietly.

The ragged stranger gave an unsteady bow. "I am known to my friends and colleagues as Jacob Rushworth, of Lynn, Massachusetts. Not six months ago I ate off bone china and drank India tea. Euclid and plane geometry were my playing field. I was a schoolmaster."

Indeed, I was embarrassed at the first estimate I had taken of this poor soul. Now I could discern in this ragged, sweat-bleached figure the outlines of former dignity.

"And you'll be master of a school again," I suggested.

"Triangles will still have three sides," suggested Ben.

Our new friend gave a weary laugh at our attempts at consolation. He leaned close, like a man telling a secret. "I have ten dollars' worth of gold dust in my pocket," he confided. "And the people back home expect me to come back rich."

In an age when any laboring man could make a dollar a day, this was a disappointing amount.

Jacob Rushworth lowered his voice, and sobriety began to creep across him, his face assuming the contemplative look of a man drunk only on regret. "But to make matters worse, in Sacramento City," he said, "they have more than gold fever—they suffer from a plague."

Dr. Merrill had set down his medical bag. Now he folded his arms.

"I saw a room full of dead men," said Jacob Rushworth, growing more sure that he had our full attention, "stretched out in rows. Rendered lifeless—by disease."

"It's easy for rumors to have a life of their own," said Dr. Merrill dismissively, but unable to fully disguise the concern in his voice.

"I saw it strike doctors, too," said the schoolmaster. "One day they'd be stepping along as lively as you. The next morning, they'd be stretched out stiff on the floor, thieves stealing the nuggets from their pockets."

Not bothering to hide his impatience, Dr. Merrill probed for a moment in his pocket, and pressed a gold eagle dollar into the former teacher's hand.

"Every one of you," croaked the schoolmaster as we left him behind, "will look death in the eye."

·⊰[CHAPTER 10]⊱·

The shop's proprietor was a tall, brown-skinned man in a broad leather belt and tight-fitting yellow pants, a dashing figure. He gave a nod to Ben and me, and a bow to Dr. Merrill, who, in his expensive silk waistcoat, managed to look every inch the gentleman.

The proprietor's English was heavily accented. It was like hearing one's familiar language through a rippling atmosphere, the sounds both distorted and beautified. He suggested a drink he called *chichi*, the fresh juice of the sugarcane, followed by a dish of the fish he had personally purchased from the fishing fleet. He enumerated the varieties of sea fish on his fingers. "We have mackerel, gentlemen, and we have both bonitos and shrimp."

I did not recognize these varieties of sea life. I was

starving for a beefsteak, but Dr. Merrill said that he had heard that the bonito was "the queen of fish."

"The king, sir," corrected the shopkeeper amiably. "The very king of sea fish."

The proprietor's daughter was a dimpled young woman, her shoulders covered in a shawl fastened with a brooch. She was pretty, in her modest dress, and Ben gave her one of his radiant smiles.

"The ladies always take a liking to Ben," I explained for Dr. Merrill's benefit.

"It fills Willie with purest jealousy," said Ben with a wink, "that they scarcely give him a look."

I didn't dare respond to that—it was too close to the truth.

I sampled the *chichi* and gave a happy nod, at which Ben drank his straight down. I was wary, after having seen what ardent spirits and tropical heat could do to someone like Mr. Rushworth. But this drink contained little, if any, in the way of alcohol. It was both cool and sweet, with a residue of pulp at the bottom of the cup when the drink was quaffed. Dr. Merrill tasted a little of the *chichi,* and then asked for a bottle of rum.

Bonito is a delicious fish, not as pale-fleshed as cod, and more meaty. Ben and I dined with pleasure, and even ate a form of vegetable our proprietor explained was called plantain, a white-fleshed starchy vegetable that fries up golden brown and which he sprinkled with lime juice.

The doctor ate well, but not as heartily as the two of

us. While Ben entertained me with stories of long-ago pirate raids on this historic town, Dr. Merrill kept a polite expression on his face, drank rum, sucked on portions of green lime, and for a long while said little.

Ben and I agreed it was the best meal we had eaten in our lives, although I realized as soon as I had said this that I was forgetting Aunt Jane's cooking, fine roasts of chicken and beef. I was also overlooking the meals I had eaten with Reverend Josselyn and Elizabeth, mallard and pheasant a local shopkeeper claimed to be "fruits of the fowling piece," but which I had always suspected had been caught in snares.

"It's a blessing for Mr. Sweetland," said Ben, "that he was traveling with a doctor."

Dr. Merrill gave a thoughtful smile. "Any wound in the torso invites sepsis."

Ben had been leaning forward, bright with apparent faith in Dr. Merrill's skill. Now he sank back in his chair. "But you sold Mr. Sweetland a pint of liver tonic."

"May his liver, in any event, remain sound," said Dr. Merrill.

Ben tried to ask the question as though the answer mattered little to him. "What sort of plague do you suppose troubles the miners?"

"Perhaps *plague* isn't the word I would use," said the doctor.

"What would you call it?" asked Ben.

If you didn't know Ben well, you'd mistake his sunny countenance as one easily deceived. Ben was the one who used a dictionary to inform me they called the California nuggets placer gold after the Spanish verb for *to please*.

"Maybe you would call it *pestilence*," suggested Ben, with just a touch of pepper in his voice.

I offered an attempt at humor, putting on a scholarly voice and intoning, "What is the exact meaning, gentlemen, of the phrase *every one of you will look death in the eye?*"

Ben laughed, but not loudly.

"I believe it's time," said the doctor with something like a smile, "that we sought livelier entertainment."

Afternoon cool filtered through the shadows as we followed Dr. Merrill down a long, cobbled lane.

The doctor bought cigars, which he shared with the two of us. Speaking an amalgam of French—which any educated gentleman knew—and simple Spanish, he inquired from one shop to another, asking questions I could not begin to understand.

I was unused to smoking cigars, although I had taken to chewing tobacco since leaving home. A cigar takes more mental effort, making sure the smoke draws well and that the ashes don't spill on your shirtfront. And there is always a certain awareness of the figure one is presenting, a man-of-the-world jauntiness that can keep the smoker from observing his surroundings too closely.

I became aware, however, of a certain tawdry cheer in the streets we now wandered. Beautiful women leaned in the doorways and made soft noises with their tongues, the way some people attract the attention of their favorite cat.

Ben leaned against a lime-washed wall near one of these brightly clad women and said something in Spanish, flashing one of his smiles.

He got a smile right back in return, and only when I tugged at his arm would he break off conversation.

I asked what he had said to these dazzling, strangely alluring women, and he said, "Something poetical out of a book. Something in Spanish about starlight, wine, and dark eyes."

"And what," I ventured with both heat and curiosity, "did they say to you?"

Ben laughed.

"You let them toy with you, Ben," I said.

"Certainly not," he protested, with a show of false innocence.

"All a woman has to do," I continued, "is roll her eyes at you, and you're a puddle at her feet."

"I'll start calling you Reverend Willie," said Ben, with more than a touch of impatience in his voice.

Dr. Merrill was waving us through a large door.

Lamps illuminated our passage down coral-stone steps. Through the atmosphere of cheroot smoke I smelled feathers, a cloying dustiness in the atmosphere, and the ammoniac tang of bird droppings.

Most of all the odor of sweat and liquor struck me as we descended into a room. A crowd of men yelled, howling in several languages, gazing down at a pit soaked in blood.

·⊰[CHAPTER 11]⊱·

Two scarlet-and-blue roosters were circling each other, the spurs of the claws already stained red.

Feathers spun about them like scythes, and soft stars of feather down floated in the air. The two cocks stalked each other in a caricature of the jauntiness I had been feeling not long before, their heads held just so, each stride a jerky, self-aware swagger.

A blur of feathers, and a struggling, confused tangle of wings broke up with both roosters sprawling. One of them flapped his wings, not to fly but to swing himself up off the wet, clawed soil. The brilliant, iridescent creature's tail feathers shook, beautiful ink-blue arcs of plumage.

But only after a long moment was it clear that the stiff-legged march the cock recommenced was following a frantic course. The bird's head was at an angle, and as each step took the rooster from the center of the cockpit, the head disengaged a little further from the spine. By the time the rooster began circling crazily, the head was dangling upside down from the spouting hole of its neck.

Ben shook his head at the sight of this carnage, and the doctor rolled his eyes.

"Keep your pennies in your pockets," called the doctor through the din, "until we go next door."

Now we crowded our way into a wide room, less raucous but nevertheless filled with Americans. A courtyard beyond held a splashing fountain, and a large, thick-branched tree, glossy leaves reflecting lantern light. In the center of the room was a roulette wheel, which I recognized from stories about the evils of gambling.

I had wagered twice in my life. Once was in a horse race along Maybeck's Green, when the filly Athena's Glory beat the entire field at the summer fair. Even Aunt Jane had placed a bet that day, and her sporting bid hardly counted as gambling. The other, more illicit bet was at a prizefight, a sport frowned on by the law.

Jack Tiernan of Boston had fought Mike Ryan, late of County Mayo, for over two hours, until the bout was stopped by the police. While both bare-fisted fighters were beaten bloody—so badly I had to close my eyes at times—and Tiernan looked about ready to drop, all bets were off because of the interruption.

I had sworn off gambling. I had made my oath on Holy Scripture, just one week after my confession to Aunt Jane that I had gone to an illegal sporting event. I believe that a sworn oath is a vow a man simply cannot break. I did, however, recognize that betting on the turning of a brilliant wheel, or the turn of a card, was by no means as low as gambling on the life and death of a pathetic, drunken bird.

"Show me how to play this game," Ben was saying over the din.

I decided to seek adventure elsewhere.

I found it soon enough.

·⊰{ CHAPTER 12 }⊱·

I breathed more easily when I was out in the soft air of the street once more, leaving the doctor and Ben to their sport.

Maybe Ben was right. Maybe I was turning into a stiff-necked sort—Reverend Willie indeed!

Nevertheless, I relished my solitude. The air was pleasantly warm, and from the gently glowing interiors drifted laughter. A Spanish song, lilting and sweet, made me believe I could understand the lovely foreign verses. And perhaps I almost could, discerning longing and love in the verdant rhymes.

I don't know how long I stood there, puffing on the remnant of my cigar. I let the stub fall into a puddle, where it sizzled and gave off a faint ghost of smoke in the muted dark. I had set forth on this journey toward the goldfields with a definite, very determined purpose, and once again the world I was traveling through took me by surprise.

I took a step up the street, startled out of my tobacco-induced reverie. I cocked my head.

There it was again, that sound.

Someone groaning.

When I saw Jacob Rushworth, he was lying beside an ivy-laced wall.

He was muttering in his drunken daze, groaning, his face lit by a candle in a nearby window. A shadow worked at his clothing, a hand darting, searching. As I approached, a figure ran, leaving Mr. Rushworth's trouser pocket cut wide open.

I ran hard after the thief, without wasting a breath in calling out. I suspected that this at last was one of the Spanish-speaking bandits we had been fearing so long, and that my shouted demands would fall on uncomprehending ears.

The thief was nimble, splashing through puddles, startling a row of tethered mules, racing along stone church steps. He led me deeper and deeper through the angling streets of the sprawling, night-sodden town.

And I ran right behind him.

·◄[CHAPTER 13]►·

We sprinted through the slumped, vine-ravaged remains of old walls.

A mound of charred sugarcane gave off a sick-sweet perfume, and a large stone wheel gleamed in the starlight, crusted with the remnants of sugar stalks. In the darkness a billy goat shied from the fugitive, and as I sprinted past, the animal made a tentative complaint, turned and tried to run, kept in place by an invisible tether.

The thief glanced back—a pale, thin face in the starlight. I ran even harder. But as we approached the edge of the jungle, roughly tilled fields and sleepy shacks, I began to grow uncertain. My quarry was not far ahead of me—I had been able to keep the pace.

But we were heading toward three or four lamps hanging in a clearing, and I had a shadowy impression of a smoking campfire, figures crouching, perhaps a dozen men along with a few women.

I put my hand on my knife handle, even though this gesture caused me momentarily to shift my pace and lose ground behind the fleet, slightly built thief. I resumed my steady stride again when the blade was in my grip, unwilling to enter a camp of strangers without a weapon drawn and ready.

Wide as my open hand, with a gently curving cutting edge, the blade was long and heavy, suited—in the words of the window advertisement—"for both the needs of the hunter and self-defense." I had bought it on Chambers Street in New York City just before hurrying off to the docks.

The knife was my most expensive possession. Some men paid as much as four hundred dollars for the trip to San Francisco, with a complete treasure-hunting kit of picks, shovels, and gold pans thrown in. Ben and I had signed on for less than a third of that, because we didn't need mining equipment, and were willing to help load trunks into the ship's hold.

But despite my heavy knife, I was beginning to doubt the extent of my allegiance to Mr. Rushworth. The derelict schoolmaster's troubles were not exactly mine, and his manner that afternoon had been less than completely polite. I was tasting the beginnings of real apprehension as the quick-footed robber reached the edge of the camp, where lamps were hanging from the trees.

He looked back at me, his face in the steady lamp-light. And then he vanished.

Before he disappeared I had a vivid glimpse of anxious green eyes, a shapeless hat pulled low, lips parted, breathing hard. I had an impression of youth, and I realized further that he looked more like a Yankee gold seeker than a local citizen.

American voices were raised. "What's the matter? Who's after you?"

A man strode to the edge of the camp, armed with a wagon spoke.

"Who's out there?" called the man, his jaw working around a mouthful of food. He had a shock of white hair, and bristling white eyebrows.

I knelt, sweating, trying to grow invisible in the grass.

I counted at least twelve people sitting around the fire, spit sizzling among the embers. The miscreant was now obscured by the larger, lumbering bulk of these Americans—yet more gold seekers, evidently, and too poor to hire beds in a hotel.

"Show yourself," said this commanding individual, his tone one of a man accustomed to being obeyed.

I was tempted to consider myself outnumbered, and go back for Ben's support. But some power pulled me to my feet, and marched me toward the lamplight.

I took a few heartbeats to further catch my breath.

"Good evening there," said the big, white-haired man, sounding perfectly at ease now that he saw that I was alone.

I am named after a brave man, who was killed when a steamboat blew up. He had rescued a dozen women and children before he was scalded to death—and I am no particular coward.

"Sir," I said, "I believe a thief is hiding in your camp."

CHAPTER 14

The stout, white-haired man adjusted his grip on the club.

The dense evening air muted my voice, but it made the words I had just spoken all the harsher. There was a long silence, and, in the thick air, mosquitoes beginning to find the flesh of my neck and arms, I had time to study my decision to speak.

And regret it. I should have gone back and stirred Ben and the doctor from their amusements, or let Mr. Rushworth's poor purse remain with its new owner.

"I find that hard to accept," the man was saying gently, with just the slightest suggestion of challenge.

He was well-fleshed, his white hair giving him a benevolent appearance. His worn, sagging boots flapped open at the toe, and his shirt had been mended, old rips stitched and gradually fraying open again.

This evidence of household care—that a wife or sister took trouble over his tired homespun—made him look both more approachable and easier to offend. The wooden club in his capable-looking fist, and the ax in the hands of an associate who ambled forward, were the only visible weapons.

But they were weapons enough, as other well-built men stood up from around the fire, stretching and hawking, scratching, in no hurry, taking their time coming over to see who was troubling their evening quiet.

"I believe I'm right, sir," I said, but I felt that I was in the beginning of a long, losing argument.

Furthermore, I was aware of the menacing appearance I presented, the hefty twelve-dollar knife in my hand. I slipped the blade back into its sheath, but kept my hand hooked on my belt, close to the handle.

"I don't think you'd find that there are any criminals here," said the big man in the easiest manner possible. He approached, and I stood my ground. He shook my hand, and introduced himself as Nicholas Barrymore. "With a whole family of Barrymores, heading out to join my brother in the goldfields."

This was the point at which I was expected to admit my mistake, but I kept my mouth shut.

"I'm a carpenter by trade," he continued with a studied but jovial manner, "out of Elmira, New York. I've had my fill with glue and wood planes, I can tell you."

Good manners forced me to introduce myself, but as

I spoke I kept trying to glance around the burly family chief, toward the campfire.

"Maybe you'd like to join us," said the man with a Sunday-morning smile I could make out even in the bad light. "We don't have much in the way of drink and victuals. Bandits took most of our supplies. But sit with us and have a cup of coffee."

The bandits must have been a bold, heavily armed gang, I nearly said.

Nicholas chuckled, perhaps reading my thoughts. "Oh, we cut a piece or two out of the robbers, don't worry about that."

Broad bodies interposed between me and the camp, with its tumble of frying pans and pots, and yet I sensed the extra presence in their midst, someone hiding. The thief's companions blocked my view, but I could see exactly where the criminal was, among the remnants of johnnycakes, fried pats of cornmeal, and a large, rust-pocked coffeepot. A new stranger—a gaunt, black-bearded man—sauntered over, his hand on his hip, where a knife nearly as long as mine was thrust naked through his belt.

I thanked Nicholas for the offer. A cup of the sweet, thick coffee Elizabeth and I used to drink together would have been most welcome just then. "Perhaps some other time," I added, sounding as polite as possible under the circumstance.

I turned on my heel, and walked away.

My nape tingled with both the whispering of mosquitoes and the expectation that with every step, there within sight of a remote, plaintively bleating goat, a heavy club was about to strike me down.

Someone was calling my name, and I ran toward the sound. I covered ground all the more quickly, having an excuse to run fast.

·⇥{ CHAPTER 15 }⇤·

A smudge in a gray shirt and gray trousers resolved, as I hurried toward it, into the most welcome sight I had ever seen.

Ben said he had been certain that bandits, or at least a panther, had dragged me away.

When Ben heard the story of the fugitive, he said, "Willie, we don't have time to catch a robber." Sometimes Ben assumes that because he reads books about botany and wild animals, he is much wiser than I am. He adopted a tone of aggrieved patience when he added, "Dr. Merrill needs us."

I was less enthusiastic to return to Dr. Merrill than I might have expected. His secretiveness, and his choice of sport for the night, had made me, for the moment, cool toward my medical acquaintance.

But I walked quickly through the trailing vines and low-hanging branches with my friend, until we stood in a room like a stone jailhouse—bare earthen floors and white-painted walls. Smoking candles illuminated the stricken men in rows along the walls, the stink of dysentery in the air.

Dr. Merrill stepped with labored care through the groaning, feverish patients of this improvised hospital. It took him a long time, and I made every effort to draw only shallow breaths. As the doctor approached us, he raised a nearly empty bottle of local rum to his lips.

"There are men like this in every hotel in the city," he said, unsteady on his feet, but his words as precise as ever. "I received word from Dr. Hauser as I was about to teach Ben here the joys of filling an inside straight." The obscure poker term struck me as devilish and frivolous under the circumstances. "The hospital is filling up rapidly. I need you and Ben to bring sick men here."

I was tired. My feet were sore. Some tonic or other would bring these men to life overnight. I wanted to lie down on a cot somewhere and close my eyes.

"This isn't just another plague, is it?" Ben was saying. "This isn't some unknown pestilence with no name."

"These men are suffering profound fevers," said the doctor, by way of answer, "and what medical books call rice-water stools."

I had heard more than enough already.

"Their diarrhea is so severe," said Dr. Merrill, examining the contents of his rum bottle in the smoky light, "that their intestinal lining is wrung out of them, in little bits that resemble grains of starch."

"It's cholera," said Ben in a whisper.

The doctor did not deny it.

⫷ CHAPTER 16 ⫸

The *California* departed Panama City before noon.

Her side wheel thrashed the water, stirring it until it was the color of coffee from silt at the bottom of the harbor. Hundreds of Americans stood on the wharf, waving and cheering halfheartedly, full of hope that another ship would soon set forth for San Francisco.

Captain Wood had allowed the steamship her full complement of passengers, more than three hundred—already too many for the ship to safely carry—and then allowed nearly one hundred more to clamber up the gangway, hauling trunks and staggering under overstuffed bags.

Dr. Merrill raised his hat from among the crowd looking up at us from the wharf, giving us as much of a smile as he could manage—he was eager to return to his patients. His small hospital had swelled with patients overnight, and he assured us that he would sail in a week or two, if a ship was available.

As we had boarded the steamship, the doctor had pressed a flask into my hands. "Dutch gin," he had said. "Some praise *genever* as a tonic. You and Ben take a hearty drink of it at the first signs of a fever." The flask was pewter, and fit snugly in the inner pocket of my coat, right over my heart.

The word that cholera had been confirmed had not caused panic so much as a determined desire to leave for California at once. Everyone had already guessed that this deadly illness, long the scourge of frontier villages, had taken its place among us. To be able to name it openly was a relief. We had all expected hazards along the journey, and people in towns and cities died of cholera without the least opportunity for adventure.

We were all quite relieved, however, to be departing the jungle.

To my happy surprise, Aaron Sweetland continued to show increasing signs of life. Mr. Gill and Mr. Kerr, the lens grinder, handled Mr. Sweetland down into steerage, strapped into a stretcher. Mr. Cowden, the rotund former law student, hovered nearby, keeping overeager fellow passengers from stumbling into the patient.

Aaron smiled up at me, reaching out his one good hand, and his touch was neither warm nor cold, his fever past. His pupils were huge—the opiates that sustained him and kept him from pain gave him a mild, almost saintly countenance.

Aaron gave my hand the ghost of a squeeze, and croaked, "We're off to the Golden Shore!"

I agreed that indeed we were. Smoke billowed from the tall, shiny black smokestack, and the Stars and Stripes lifted languorously over our wake. Cinders from the smokestack bit our skin and made our eyes smart.

Stewards descended into the steerage, to help arrange the stowing of mining equipment and clothing. They answered complaints that there ought to be laws against such overcrowding with reasonable humor, and generally held their own against an excited, eager crowd that did not look likely to sleep much during the passage anyway.

The great vessel began to heave slowly from side to side, and plunged deliberately into the brine, the ocean swells carrying her now. As waves misted over us, the men enjoyed a promenade on deck. At times we were so jammed together, we were unable to turn around without apologizing for treading on a boot.

The last outline of land sank to the east.

At twilight of the first day Nicholas Barrymore bumped into me along the rail. The sight of him brought my hand to the handle of my knife, an involuntary gesture.

It was not lost on him—he crinkled his eyes in a

knowing smile. I wanted to ask him if he'd managed to get all of his kin and equipment on board—frying pans, kettles, and thieves. But instead I simply wished him a good evening, like any gentleman out for a promenade downtown, and he greeted me likewise in return.

I told him that I worked with my hands, too, repairing carriages and guns. "I can do a bit of carpentry, too," I allowed.

"I'll take my chances shoveling Sierra gravel," he said amiably. "But I respect a young man who can use his hands."

"Your entire family is going to the gold country?" I asked, still determined to root out the identity of the thief.

"Every one of them," he said. "All but the family dog. The poor mutt died on the way."

I made a remark regarding last night's offer of a cup of coffee.

"That will be something to look forward to," he said, cordially enough. "We'll have a good sit-down talk—when we have the space to stretch out and feel at home." He looked me in the eye, both kindly and deeply amused. "Willie, I don't mind telling you that some of my children are little better than rascals."

"I'm sorry to hear it." Nevertheless, I couldn't help feel a stab of compassion for this family man, keeping his tribe fed and out of trouble on this long journey.

"They are rascals and rapscallions," he said with an air of cheerful meditation. "But good-hearted young people, nonetheless."

"I have no reason to doubt it," I said. Politeness forced me to exaggerate my faith in his family's character, but I found myself liking this man and his kin despite myself.

"I would stay out of their way, though, Willie—if I were you," said Mr. Barrymore. "Don't ask too many questions."

"I beg your pardon," I responded with more than a little spirit. I don't care to be threatened.

He put a hand out to my arm, with every show of good nature. "What father can tell his children not to sin, and be certain they'll follow his counsel?"

Something likable about Mr. Barrymore, some warmth in his nature, continued to keep me from being completely annoyed by him—or intimidated. He was a heavily clawed, shaggy beast who, without ceasing to be a predator, was capable of real friendliness.

"If I were you," cautioned the white-haired family man with a chuckle, "I'd stay out of their way."

In the forthcoming days I met every manner of person.

Men reading volumes of Lord Byron or tuning a violin, men gambling at cards, and some men temporarily paralyzed with hard drink. But my mind kept traveling back to the Barrymores. I found them fascinating, for reasons I could not have named.

I spied the dark-whiskered man with the long, naked Bowie knife, but I did not see the thief again.

Not yet.

···❧ CHAPTER 17 ❧···

A touch of coolness had slipped into my friendship with Ben.

We shared a brief sip of Dutch tonic from the pewter flask from time to time, as a defense against illness, but I decided to conserve the liquor, not certain what plagues we might face in the future. Perhaps this touch of abstemiousness annoyed Ben. He was still keen to tell me the names of sea life—porpoises, sharks, and a broad, smooth-skinned creature he said was a ray-fish. But Ben was full of ideas—whether to search for the ore by hand, or find some profitable occupation, one that would earn the wealth that had been discovered by others.

I still tried to maintain that my major interest in voyaging to California was to find the man who had wronged Elizabeth. It was no longer entirely true. Hour by hour I was beginning to succumb as well, gold fever simmering in my heart. I was as eager as any man to set foot in San Francisco, and find a land or river route up into the Sierra foothills where, even now, men from around the world were digging fortunes right out of the ground.

Perhaps I was a little envious at the easy way in which Ben found an audience, reciting sonnets and scenes from Shakespeare. Educated and unlettered men alike enjoyed hearing a bit of high culture, and Ben was satisfied to respond—and he was good at it, giving the words just the right color. You could listen to Ben for hours and never get tired.

On the other hand, I could read a man his own death warrant and make it sound dull.

The ship's beef was so tough—and so close to being rotten—that men protested at being served their first portion, certain that some joke was being offered at their expense. Even when we realized that this leathery, rancid fiber was to be standard fare during the voyage, we ate the stuff with a semblance of humor. My fellow voyagers became clever at ruses that improved the food, such as sinking a slice of bread in a weak mixture of rum and water, and waiting as the weevils abandoned the bread only to drown.

It was possible for a steamer to navigate all the way

to San Francisco in well under two weeks—there was talk of ten-day voyages, and even shorter passages. Our voyage, however, was punctuated by a delay off the coast of Mexico. A wood boat out of Mazatlan was scheduled to meet us, but the vessel did not arrive for many hours, while the seas around us grew ugly, laced with froth. Waves crashed over the prow as the side wheel churned to keep us in place. When the wood boat arrived, it was too dangerous for the bargelike craft to approach until late that night, when, in the darkness, the heavy seas subsided.

Early morning saw ship's boys gathering gnarled fragments of fuel wood from the deck. Within hours, our first burial at sea took place, within sight of the low hills of the Mexican mainland. A law clerk from New York, this cholera victim was given a solemn burial, the captain officiating.

No one dared to utter the name of the illness, no doubt praying that some heart ailment or chronic dropsy was to blame for this fatality.

One night a voice was lifted in song, the hymn about the Rock of Ages.

It was Aaron Sweetland, singing again, his strength nearly fully returned.

People from all over the world were pouring into California, by all accounts, and I was not certain that I would be equal to the adventure. In a world of brawn and energy, I was not sure that the habits of steadiness that I had learned repairing harnesses and flintlocks would serve me well on the Golden Shore.

The two weeks passed. I believed at times that this span of days would never end. Each day was the same, identical twenty-four hours, the same daylight and nighttime repeating over and over, land a faint ghost way off to the east as we steamed north, cinders raining down on us from the smokestack. Only the weather altered, very slightly, fading from robust tropical sun to something less ardent, sunlight slipping from cloud to cloud.

Perhaps I expected some ceremony, or an announcement from the captain.

The wind had been growing colder, but the sun was still pleasantly warm as we steamed along a coast of distant cliffs and trees. Men had been whispering, checking and rechecking their mining equipment, shovels brought out and then packed again with the picks and hoes and other tools the shipping companies had sold at a premium.

One minute we were churning north.

The next the vessel was heading eastward, the side wheel churning, bits of charcoal falling all the more thickly from the smokestack. We made our way into the waters of a large inlet, tall hills to the north, and a low, sandy shore to the south. Men crowded the starboard rail, already laden with their traveling bags.

Ben turned to find me in the pack of people against the rail, his eyes ablaze with excitement.

We had reached the Golden Gate and we were moment by moment closer to San Francisco.

PART TWO
BLOOD

·•⦂[CHAPTER 18]⦂•·

A year or two before, this city had been a sleepy out-post, a Franciscan mission and a sparse village with a view of empty bay and distant hills. Since the days of the conquistadors, California had been a remote Spanish territory, and then, with Mexican independence in the 1820s, a peaceful province of vast rancheros and poppy fields belonging to Mexico.

Now San Francisco's harbor was a crowded tangle of sailing ships, two or three hundred vessels. The skele-tons of naked masts and spars resembled a wintry wood. No sailors worked these ships and, save for the creaking grind of hull against hull, nearly all were dead quiet.

"They are all abandoned," said a ship's boy, spitting tobacco juice over the side. "Their crews are off striking it rich."

A small steamer, spewing sulfuric smoke, towed us

toward the dock, bits of coal grit raining down on us from the diminutive pilot boat. I realized that this was where the *California* had received the since-repainted scratches along her hull, forcing her way through the abandoned fleet.

The wharf was a bustling maze of coffee sacks and wooden crates. I had a glimpse through the crowd the gangway disgorged onto the docks of Mr. Gill and Mr. Sweetland, Aaron carrying one arm in a dirty yellow sling and smiling, Mr. Kerr and Mr. Cowden half buried under baggage.

Then we were lost in the flood of new arrivals. A longshoreman looked right through me—I was invisible. I tried to give him a look right back, unsteady on my legs because of our voyage. A man in a top hat, the first such headgear I had seen in a long while, introduced himself as a hotel agent, and said he could supply "accommodations of every variety."

Neither Ben nor I spoke to the gentleman, not because we were discourteous, but because we were momentarily stunned at the scene. The top-hatted gent abandoned us with a tip of his hat, and his business offer was repeated to one disembarking passenger after another.

I was so accustomed to the dependable, if crowded, nature of shipboard life that the stewing noise of the street bewildered me. I put out a hand to steady my frame on Ben's shoulder. The buildings along the street were brick, with balconies overlooking a scene hectic with men in a hurry, calling out to each other, clutching papers or valises, no one simply walking along, every individual in a rush. Even the men who labored under loads of sea trunks, helping passengers who had come to an agreement with a hotel agent, went quickly, bent under their loads.

I made an effort to appear unimpressed, making our way down the middle of the street, each of us carrying one end of our sea-trunk. But this wasn't an easygoing sort of town, and it was hard to appear carefree holding up one end of a steamer trunk.

A violent crash froze us.

···≼ CHAPTER 19 ≽···

One wagon collided with another, so close to us that a splinter hit Ben's hat and stuck there.

The iron wheels locked, and the wooden fellies—the rims just under the iron—broke with a load crack. Spokes popped out, both wagons instantly crippled, and both Ben and I were surrounded by bits of wagon spokes and shouting men.

I had spent long hours in the carriage shop on Harrison Street shaping such ash or white oak spokes with a drawshave. I used to help quench the wheels, heating the iron rim and lowering it sizzling and spitting into water. I used to paint the fine red lines on the spokes and polish the brass lamps on either side of the driver's seat. I helped fit the best Norway iron onto the hub collars, and in every way came to love carriages and wagons.

I hated to see the sudden wreck that chance had made of two serviceable, if inelegant, mud wagons. Both wagon drivers set their brakes, by habit, brakes being only partially useful in such a situation, and climbed down into the street. Each driver had assistants, boys in oversized, floppy caps, with dirty, hard-looking hands, evidently traveling to help load freight. These helpers leaped down to the muddy street, their fists bunched and ready for a fight.

Both drivers were equipped with whips. Wagon spokes lay strewn about, and the mules shied nervously, lifting up their hooves and gingerly putting them down the way animals do when they want to run away but are forced to stay put. But the moment of greatest tension seemed about to pass without a blow being struck.

Without a word of command, the assistants eased the two wagons apart as one of the mules laid back his ears and took a chomp out of a sleeve. Observers laughed, and I had the hopeful intuition that everything was going to be all right.

It was not the first time I had been badly mistaken.

The two drivers had plenty of help, men gathering spokes, assistants heaving the wheel rims over to the buildings, where several chairs lined up along the street allowed a few gentlemen a view of the ongoing tumult. One of the drivers, a big man with a bald head and a flowing blond beard, declared, "I don't like to see a drunken poltroon handle a team of mules in a city street."

Poltroon is the basest sort of coward, and I could not

see how lack of courage had anything at all to do with the mishap. The remark had been made as though to the surrounding, cigar-smoking observers.

But the words were just loud enough so the opposing driver—a tall, clean-shaven man—could not keep from hearing them.

The tall driver's jaw worked angrily at the tobacco in his mouth. He continued examining his mules, and checking over the harness, bending down to observe the singletree under the wagon. Cordial voices called out for the two drivers to calm down and get the wrecks out of the street. A burly man with a gray beard and a businessman's gray frock coat strode down out of a shop and said, "Let's hurry up and get these wagons out of the way."

I stepped in to lend a hand with one of the wagons, which were badly balanced on their three wheels and beginning to teeter. Ben joined in with the attempts to keep the adjoining wagon from falling over. There was still one mule in a troubled mood. The angry animal showed its teeth again, and lunged at the gray-coated businessman. The mule's harness jangled, and the white teeth snapped together with an instant corona of mule sweat and spit. The gray-clad man wheeled his arms as he retreated, staggering, bystanders breaking his fall.

But we were too many, too close together, and two men tumbled backward, puddles splashing. I was one of them.

I landed hard on my rear end.

I sat there feeling embarrassed, but aware that no one was taking any special notice of me. I was about to hoist my body up off the street, when a well-polished boot struck my ribs, and a large body tumbled on top of me.

The breath was shocked right out of my body, an elbow in my chest.

"God damn it," said a strong male voice, his chin right beside my ear.

He picked himself up.

"God damn it," he repeated, looking down at his trouser knees, which were wet, and gazing critically at a streak of street spatter along one sleeve.

He was a neatly mustached, square-jawed man in a black frock coat and a top hat, which had been knocked forward onto his forehead by his collision with me. He removed his hat, examined its shiny black brim, and resettled it on his head.

He was far more concerned with his hat than with me, but as he adjusted his clothing he exposed a pistol tucked into his waistcoat pocket. This was the sort of small pistol with a large bore most people keep at home in a rosewood case.

Ben gave me his hand and helped me to my feet.

"Are you hurt, my friend?" the gentleman asked warmly.

I said that of course I was not hurt, not wanting to have anything to do with this armed stranger.

"You're bleeding," Ben confided to me.

My teeth had bit into my lip, and I spat some blood

onto the rutted, muddy street. A small speck of the blood flew wide, and splashed on the toe of the gentleman's boot. He said, with every evidence of trying to remain patient, "For God's sake."

I was sure that I had made a fatal mistake. I had walked right into this city full of bustle and violence, encountered a man who carried what was probably a loaded pistol—and I insulted him by spitting on his boot.

"My apologies, sir," I said, my voice breathless. I tried to take comfort in the weight of my knife at my hip.

He was still not satisfied with his hat, taking it off, readjusting it.

"Please do accept my apology, sir," I offered again.

"We're just in from Panama City," said Ben. "On the steamer *California*, fourteen days' passage." He beamed, making such a display of friendly conversation that I felt thankful for my friend's breezy good cheer.

"In Panama City they have more bandits than rats," I exaggerated, implying that Ben and I had hacked our way through an army of armed and desperate men. My intention was to make us sound tough, and not appear to be a couple of rank novices.

The man showed his teeth, white and even under his mustache, and smiled as he said, "Oh, in California we have cannibal-bandits, an entire army of them. They roast up their victims, and serve them in a kind of chowder."

Ben gave an easy laugh, but I never know what to do when I'm being made the object of rough humor.

"Nevertheless," continued the gentleman thoughtfully, "two young men fresh from the jungle may prove useful."

The clean-shaven driver was sorting out his reins, and I stepped over to hold the nervous mule steady, speaking soothingly to the sweating animal. Already dray-company boys were fitting on new wheels, with the help of mechanically gifted bystanders, but the animals were still quite unhappy. The bearded driver's animals shook their harness and he swore at them, but the clean-shaven driver was the picture of professionalism.

Perhaps my willingness to help calm the mules resolved some question in the gentleman's mind. Ben and I stooped to heft our steamer trunk out of the way of a dray wagon full of barrels, but the armed stranger put a hand to the pistol in his pocket, perhaps to check that his weapon was still there, and gave a sharp whistle. Four boys gathered, each dirty but looking both well-fed and eager. They all seemed to know him, and were anxious to help.

It was hard to read the intention behind the stranger's smile when he looked back at us and said, "You're coming with me."

···❧ CHAPTER 20 ❧···

As we walked through the hectic streets, he gave us handsomely engraved cards that announced him as "Horatio Castleman, New York and London, theatricals."

He sat us down in the dining room of the Hotel Olympian and ordered steak and potatoes for the two of us, with champagne being served at the astonishingly high price of one dollar per glass. The dining room was too filled with laughter and boasting in several languages for much conversation among the three of us. Every time we tried to shout out some polite comment, Mr. Castleman would smile and cup his ears with his hands, and shake his head. The amount of noise was prodigious, as was the speed with which food was both served up and eaten, forks scraping against dishes, wine glasses clinking.

Mr. Castleman enjoyed a few oysters along with his champagne, but Ben and I were hungry beyond anything I had ever experienced. My beefsteak was succulent and huge, with potatoes sliced and fried, so much the way Aunt Jane used to fix them that I blinked tears of memory and gratitude.

After the conclusion of our meal, puffing on fine little cigars, we strode quickly in Mr. Castleman's wake, down one alley, and up another, until we had reached a back staircase, so recently painted the white surface was tacky.

It was a rambling house, with unoccupied side rooms right beside chambers fully decorated with furnishings. Each room smelled of freshness. We found ourselves now in one such sunny sitting room, carpeted and featuring the statue of a nymph or other wood maiden in a state of undress. The chairs were upholstered with what I recognized as the finest chintz, and a plush footstool stood beside an elegantly polished cuspidor. Our trunk had arrived before us, and sat there on the fine purple rug.

"I gather, Willie," said Mr. Castleman, applying a silver-handled clothes brush to the sleeves of his coat, "that you have some experience in handling livestock."

I agreed that I could manage a team, up to six horses, and added that I dreamed of running a carriage shop some day.

"And you can use a knife," he added, with a glance at the blade at my belt.

"He'll skin a thief alive," said Ben, "if he has a chance."

Mr. Castleman poured a glass of port wine for each of us, and then set to work on his boots with an ivory-chased brush.

I allowed that I had some experience as a gunsmith, but added, "I would rather work on carriage springs than firearms."

"You're a man of peace, Willie?" said Mr. Castleman.

"Guns don't work very well, in my view," I said. "Even most rifles are badly made, with a fixed sight, so you can't elevate the sight to adjust for distance." I didn't want to mention the danger of shooting the wrong person in the dark.

As he finished brushing his boots, Mr. Castleman explained that California was as yet a bleak but promising place for a man of culture. "But I'm doing all I can to repair that condition."

The dark wine stung my lip, which began bleeding again. Mr. Castleman handed me a bit of gun wadding, the sort of soft cloth used to tamp down musket loads. This convinced me further that I was in the presence of a gentleman of potential violence, and I determined to make no foolish remark, or any idle talk of any kind. But at the same time I was fascinated by him.

He encouraged me to talk about Panama City, and so, warmed by a few sips of port wine, I did.

I was struck by his combination of manly directness

and generosity, and his fussiness over his belongings, his boots now gleaming again. Some people dislike a dandy. It seemed to me, however, that a man who polishes his buckle will also keep a sharp edge on a knife. I felt guarded whenever his eyes met mine, and something about the way he tilted his head, and made a great show of listening to our shabby adventures through the jungle, made me wonder how much of his charm was genuine.

So after a few remarks about snakes and jungle fever, I kept my silence. Ben conversed easily, as usual, asking, with a glance in my direction, "How hard will it be to find any particular individual up among the mines?"

Mr. Castleman poured himself another glass of port wine from the heavy crystal decanter. "There are forty thousand men up and down the Yuba and the American Rivers, some of them digging precious ore to the tune of ten thousand dollars a week. They aren't really mines, you know. They dig the nuggets and what the books call 'auriferous sands' right out of the ground."

"Have you found any gold yourself?" asked Ben.

"Ah, no, Ben—not I," replied Mr. Castleman in an air of worldly sadness. "The goldfields are all upriver from here, two or three days by schooner, and I hear that the best claims are taken. But I've seen nuggets brought into the city as big as horse apples, and there is still plenty of the yellow stuff to be had."

"William doesn't want to see a single pinch of gold dust," said Ben, a little pointedly. "He's looking for satisfaction from a man somewhere up in the foothills."

It was like Ben to embellish the truth a little. *Looking for satisfaction* meant that there were matters between us that could only be settled by a duel, with either swords or firearms. It was a dignified phrase, though, and despite the fact I wished Ben did not talk so openly to this stranger, I liked the sound of it.

"But you haven't actually seen any placer gold yet," said Mr. Castleman, a calculating glint in his eye.

"I know what the stuff looks like," I retorted. But I softened my manner and added, "We've seen very little California gold, it's true."

"We've seen none of it," said Ben.

Mr. Castleman slipped a leather pouch from his pocket, the sort used to carry pipe tobacco. He let a tiny amount of golden flakes spill out onto the plain pine table. The sound the dust made arrested me, a baritone whisper.

They were coarse grains the size of roughly ground wheat. He stirred the mineral with his finger. It was more like grains of wheat than I would have expected and less obviously shiny than everyday coins or watches. But I could not avert my eyes from it. The precious element uttered another heavy whisper on the pinewood table as Mr. Castleman soothed it flat. This was a treasure right out of Nature herself.

"They pay for theater tickets with this dust," he said huskily.

Ben's eyes were alight.

Mr. Castleman soothed the gold flakes back into his pouch.

"I took you for a pair of adventurers," said Mr. Castleman, "as soon as I set eyes on you."

The sight of the gold had stirred something in me. I felt an instant lust for the ore, an unexpected hunger to have some.

"What are you telling us?" prompted Ben.

Mr. Castleman gave us a smile. "Gentlemen, I can make you rich."

·⊰[CHAPTER 21]⊱·

Our steps echoed as we followed Mr. Castleman.

Before us, in the darkness half-abolished by steadily burning candle flames, was an expanse of empty plank flooring, closed off at one side by a heavy curtain.

Our host strode across the boards, flung open the curtain, the material of the cloth plush purple in his hands. He held the curtain open, and rows of empty seats gleamed in the half-light, wooden chairs lined up, bank upon bank.

"For three and a half months," he said, "we've dazzled men from around the world, gold seekers from Chile and France, Peru and China."

Ben and I had been in theaters many times before in Philadelphia. My favorites had been a performance of

William Shakespeare's *Hamlet*—with a rousing sword fight—and *The Killer Duke*, about a man who had many dramatic escapes. We had seen DeQuille the Wizard in the St. James's Theater on Chestnut Street. The man had worn a laced white shirtfront and had made playing cards disappear and reappear. He had a pig that would spell out words using lettered wooden blocks, and he would let the sow answer questions from the respectful audience.

The pig was as wise as any almanac, and when Ben asked if the millpond would freeze before December, the pig spelled out *If it snows*. As it happened, there was a blizzard on November 30, and you could crawl most of the way out over the pond.

"Is it usual in California," I asked, interrupting Mr. Castleman's description of the theater-going public, "for actors to carry pistols?"

"Oh, I'm not an actor," said our host, perhaps a little sadly. "But this is, there is no question, a pistol. I am a producer, manager, and artistic director of—" He gestured artfully.

"It is very grand," I admitted, remembering my manners.

I envied Mr. Castleman, despite my misgivings. In an era of scarce entertainment, both educated and uneducated folk thronged to the theater, especially here in the West. I had heard that everything from *Dr. Faustus* to the most thrill-ridden melodrama would be welcome here, and I knew why. For the price of a ticket, a traveler could view handsome women, enjoy the flights of poetry—and for a short time cure that nagging homesickness each of us felt.

"I intend to construct a portable stage," he was saying, "of pine boards and canvas, and take our show to the distant reaches of—"

"—the gold country," said Ben.

Castleman gave a nod.

"Father," interrupted a young woman's voice, "I can't get my trunk open to save my soul."

A young lady in what I took to be a dressing gown—a whispering, silken mantle—swept across the bare boards of the stage, and stopped when she caught full sight of me and my companion.

"You've found the two brutes we need," she said. "Two well-proportioned young men," she corrected herself.

I hitched at my belt and wished I had glanced in a mirror at some point earlier in the day.

Her father performed the necessary introductions. Her name was Constance, a young woman about my age and, as Mr. Castleman put it, "both Ophelia and Portia in our *Feminine Portraits from William Shakespeare,* just completing its run. My daughter," he concluded, "is gifted."

Elizabeth would have demurred, compliments making her blush.

But Constance took this praise without a change of expression. "It's my mother the audiences come to see," she said. "She performs as Sarah Encard—you may have read of her performance in *Fortune's Frolic* in New York last year."

"We're two ignorant travelers," said Ben.

Constance stepped forward, and put her hand on Ben's arm. "Two gentlemen of the world, I would suspect," she said.

Ben replied smoothly, "I have been studying the fauna and flora of the American tropics."

"Snakes and bugs," I interjected.

"Are you a naturalist, then?" Constance asked smoothly, looking at Ben appraisingly.

"Perhaps I am one, in the making," responded Ben, with a quiet little laugh. Then he added, barely glancing my way, "William here wants to fix carriage springs for a living."

"One of these capable gentlemen," added Mr. Castleman, "survived an accidental attack from me. I believe I kicked you, Mr. Dwinelle, and then I fell on you."

"It was a rough introduction," I said with what I hoped was good humor. Ben and Constance stood very close to each other.

"William fell down," Ben added, I thought unnecessarily. "And your father—" Ben made an amusing imitation of a comical collapse.

Constance laughed, a musical and, I think, much practiced sound, a trill of notes from high octave to low. I didn't like her, and I didn't like the way she was laughing again at something Ben was saying, how everyone in the street had size fourteen boots and it was a wonder they didn't all stumble and fall flat.

"I'd like to offer you a job, the two of you," said Mr. Castleman. "But first you'll need to endure an employment interview with Lady Macbeth herself."

"Father," interjected Constance, "just hire them on the spot."

"The duties involved would include helping me protect the honor," Mr. Castleman said, "of two beautiful women, and driving a carriage encumbered with theatrical equipment."

"William could drive an Abbot and Downing coach blindfolded," said Ben. Abbot and Downing made the famous Concord coaches, and most of the other coaches and wagons I both drove and repaired.

"And what can you do?" Constance inquired of Ben.

A woman's voice sounded from the darkness. "Good lord, Horatio, there's another behemoth rat in the hallway."

A larger—and even more shapely—version of Constance, likewise garbed in an almost embarrassingly intimate dressing gown, breezed onto the bare stage. "If I had something to kill it with, I'd mash it flat."

"The creatures come off the ships," said Mr. Castleman, whispering. Perhaps it was not considered polite or wise to hurt an eavesdropping rat's feelings. "All the abandoned vessels in the harbor. Thousands of rodents from all around the world, starving and curious."

"Bold," said Constance. "They stare at one, right in the face."

Her father excused himself, and drew the pistol from his inner pocket. He tiptoed in an exaggerated manner across the stage boards. I had been about to comment that I had never heard anyone praise the accuracy of such a diminutive firearm, but I kept my silence as his steps took him beyond the illumination of the few candles, and into the shadowy hallway beyond.

The tiptoed progress of Mr. Castleman continued with painful slowness, and then stopped, somewhere off in the hallway.

I held my breath, and not one of us made a move. A metallic *click-click* pierced the silence, the gun being cocked.

He must have double-cracked the gun—used twice the normal amount of gunpowder. It's a dangerous practice if the gun isn't kept in prime working order—a double load of powder can cause a firearm to burst.

The shot was very loud.

·⊰[CHAPTER 22]⊱·

"In fact," argued Ben, "I think we have an obligation to travel with these fascinating people."

"To keep Mr. Castleman," I suggested with sarcasm, "from shooting one of the ladies by mistake?"

The pistol ball had made short work of the rat, which I had volunteered to dispose of in the back alley. I had stretched the deceased rodent respectfully on the ground where, judging by the growls, a pair of dogs quarreled over it as soon as I made my way up the steps.

Ben had several different smiles, and this one meant: I'm waiting patiently for you to be serious.

For the moment I made no further argument. My ears had stopped ringing from the pistol shot at last. We had just visited our third shipping company, looking for the name Ezra Nevin on the books. The clerks had been businesslike and crisp—the rosters were not for just anyone to look at. One clerk went so far as to say, "I couldn't let my own brother look at these books."

We wandered Sansome Street, the place so crowded that men bumped into us as they made their way across the muddy street, barely calling back an apology.

"We can't let those two ladies and that dandified man," said Ben, "travel upriver without help."

"Especially the ladies," I said dryly.

"They need our attentions, Willie, don't you think?"

A row of chairs had been set out along the street, and men sat there, watching the to-and-fro of the crowd in the street. The chairs were all occupied, but I took my place among them, watching the spectacle of hundreds of men walking too fast to wish each other a good evening, every man angling off in an independent direction. There was a long line of men at an office that sold tickets to Sacramento City, and even the approach of night did little to diminish the bustle around us.

I felt a very definite thrill at the excitement, but I did not care for the company of Mr. Castleman any longer. I did not trust him, and I did not like the growing friendship between Ben and Constance. She laughed musically through her nose, tilting her head back. I had never seen anything quite like it, or the way Ben brightened under her attention.

"What if we don't ever find Ezra?" my friend was saying.

"We will."

"But if we don't, Willie, what's your plan?"

The truth was, I had wondered about this. I didn't want to put words to such a fear—it might cause it to happen. And furthermore, my desire to find Ezra had weakened a good deal during our journey, especially since our arrival. So much excitement—and the promise of wealth—had made the former purpose of my trip seem dogged and lifeless.

"I think whether we find Ezra or not is not so important anymore," said Ben. He folded his arms to give his words more emphasis.

I couldn't answer him right away. I folded my arms, too.

"We didn't know what California would be like," said Ben, a new quality in his voice. "Or how exciting it would be. People are getting rich, Willie!"

He was putting into words the very thoughts that had begun to tease me, but that did not make what he was saying any more welcome. "Stay away from the daughter," I heard myself say.

"Constance?" he asked airily.

"I don't trust her."

Ben chuckled. It was a sort of artificial, humorless laugh I had never heard from him before, offhand and defensive. "And her mother," he said. "I suppose you don't care for her, either."

I was turning into Reverend Willie again.

"How will we ever," said Ben, "become men of the world?"

I had no particular goal to become such a creature, I wanted to rejoin. But I did feel suddenly small-minded and ignorant.

"Do you know why," asked Ben, "the shipping clerks won't let us look at their precious books?"

I thought for a moment. "They're following the shipping company rules."

"We're expected to bribe them," said Ben. "They want gold, just like everyone else—and we don't have any."

·❧{ CHAPTER 23 }❧·

It was hard to sleep that night.

Ben and I were stretched out on the plush furniture of the Castleman sitting room, our heads on feather-stuffed pillows. We were comfortable enough. But men in the street outside were liquored up, cheering and arguing. Some sort of contest was going on in the dark street, a footrace or a wrestling match. When the drunken competition had concluded at last, something like silence descended over the neighborhood.

Then Mr. Castleman's voice resounded through the walls. I could not make out the words, but only the distinct rise and fall of his speech, a man in love with his own voice. Now and then his wife made a sound, a reassuring murmur. She had a beautiful speaking voice, it was true. Mr. Castleman would start in again, and, for all his talk, I began to wonder if he was as confident as he wished to be. What would our duties turn out to be, I wondered? Would we help to drive a team of mules, and nail stage scenery into place? Or would we act as bodyguards in some unsavory business?

I was aware, too, of the soft steps of his daughter in the room adjoining ours.

Ben slipped into the slow, steady respiration of a sleeper. The building shook faintly when someone leaned heavily against the exterior wall of the place, and the joints and timbers of the house creaked in the wind. But I was pleased to have a bed within walls and under a roof, and before much longer I enjoyed a dreamless slumber.

A whisper woke me.

Someone had spoken.

Or was it a laugh?

Ben was gone, leaving only a tangle of blankets.

I groped through the poor light and found my knife.

·⊰[CHAPTER 24]⊱·

"There's no need to shout," said Ben.

"I am not shouting," I said, in a careful whisper, and retreated from the room.

I had not made any loud exclamation. I had taken in a sudden gasp of air, quite shocked. But as far as I was aware, no actual shout had escaped my lips.

As I returned to my blanket, I ran through the lurid images that had just confronted me: Ben half naked, Constance little better, the two of them in a stuffy, freshly painted little side room, lit by a stub of a candle.

I sat there on the floor, waiting for Ben to hurry into the room.

I was ready to entertain his protestations of innocence with an air of worldly sophistication. I would show him that I was not a man easily offended, and certainly not jealous—not at all. We were all broad-minded here in San Francisco.

It did not trouble me a bit that a young woman—who looked very much like the marble nymph in the corner of the sitting room, and in a similar state of undress—had chosen Ben as her consort.

Instead of me.

But there was still no sign of Ben.

I pulled on my boots, tucked in my shirt, found my hat. I dragged a satchel of my belongings from the steamer trunk in a room filled with tailor's dummies and wig stands, all of it giving off the odor of newness. I shouldered this satchel, not caring if Ben heard me, or anyone else.

A distant, domestic snoring sounded from what I took to be the bedchamber of Mr. Castleman and Lady Macbeth, and an odd near-silence pulsed from the shut door of the trysting place of Ben and Constance. I made a certain amount of noise on purpose. I shuffled my feet, and thumped the floor as I hefted the satchel along, all the way across the kitchen, and down the back steps to the alley.

I clumped my way down the steps and out into the alley, expecting with every step to hear Ben call after me.

He caught up with me in the street at last, an outlandish nightshirt stuffed into his trousers, a huge garment of white linen, something Hamlet might wear. His suspenders dangled, and one foot was thrust into a curl-toed Persian slipper four sizes too small. Early-morning bustle already filled the street, but no one gave Ben's costume a second glance.

"This is the opportunity of a lifetime," said Ben, in a low, urgent voice.

"Opportunity for what?" I spoke in an equally low voice, but with great feeling. "To lounge in the bedchamber of"—I made a mental effort to come up with the right phrase—"of a Delilah?"

Ben folded his arms.

I said, "You're a man of weak character, Ben."

Ben heaved his shoulders like a person trying to control his temper.

"I'm ashamed of you," I said, more sharply, perhaps, that I had intended.

Ben shook his head.

"I'm not ever going to be able to put into a letter to Elizabeth," I went on, "the things I've seen you doing on this trip."

Ben spoke after a tense silence. "Do you know why Ezra Nevin is going to be too busy to so much as speak to you, Willie?"

I knew better than to respond to a question like that.

"Because," he said, "he's a gentleman. And you're"—Ben searched for the word to deliver his judgment in all its flavor—"you're so *uncultured*!"

·⇥[CHAPTER 25]⇤·

"She's taking on water through her hull," said Captain Deerborn of the *Nyad*.

"Leaking?" I suggested.

I had been directed to this ship by a sooty, unshaven clerk. It was the first vessel bound for Sacramento City and the goldfields to leave this morning, and there was no shortage of passengers. I paused on the wharf, uncertain what I should do. A trip across San Francisco Bay, and up the Sacramento River, some one hundred miles was the most reliable route to the gold country, but I was certain every moment that I would see Ben.

"Not leaking, so much as sinking," he said with little concern, leaning forward to spit carefully over the ship's side.

It was dawn, but already the two-masted ship was crowded with trunks and passengers. The odor of fried eggs and bacon drifted over the wharves, and I was hungry as well as feeling keenly the absence of my friend.

Surely, I told myself, Ben would come running along any minute, out of breath and eager to join me.

The captain looked at me over the gunwale of the two-masted ship, taking my reluctance to embark to be evidence of quite another sort of crisis.

"If you lack money," he said, "you can work your way upriver."

I could guess what work he had in mind. "Helping to man the pumps?"

"We can use another able body," he said, in a quiet voice. He was a big man, with square head, thick neck, and massive shoulders.

I shot another glance up and down the wharf.

"Or maybe you're waiting for a certain friend," he said.

I gave a nod.

"She'll not come to see you off," he said, not unkindly. "They never do."

Nicholas Barrymore and his family were among the passengers on this crowded ship. The white-haired man gave me a friendly wave from his seat near the prow, and the dark-bearded man with the knife gave me a humorless smile from his position near the rail.

I smiled right back at him, feeling an odd relief at seeing familiar faces—even menacing ones. For some reason I felt a genuine liking for this gang of rascals. I searched the Barrymores, men and a few women, for a glimpse of that thin-faced thief. Perhaps travel makes us grateful for familiar faces, regardless of their character.

Aaron Sweetland and Isom Gill were among us, too, although most of the Tioga County Mining and Assaying Company had elected to wait for a larger boat to allow them to transport every ounce of their considerable mining equipment. I was glad to see my two former traveling companions, too, but something about the Barrymore party continued to draw my eye. Nicholas folded his arms with an air of cheerful excitement, and the thin, black-bearded man stayed at his side.

Their air of rough comradeship was welcome to me, after the confusing worldliness of the Castleman household. The Barrymores might be potentially dangerous, but it was a familiar, gritty sort of menace. Something else plucked at my attention, too—a quality about their company that I could not name.

Only as I turned to carry my satchel down the companionway did I begin to guess what it was. I hurried back on deck to verify what I had seen. There among the burly, intimidating group was someone in a gray dress, a demure, full-sleeved garment, complete with a bonnet that totally shadowed her features.

Nicholas lifted one of his white eyebrows and said something to Blackbeard.

I shifted the plug of tobacco in my cheek and made my way to the shabby, adventurous-looking family.

So they dress thieves in women's clothing in California, I was about to say—certain that I had stumbled on the truth.

111

But before I could make this challenging remark, rehearsing it over and over again in my mind, the womanly figure turned to meet me.

The words died in my mouth.

Nicholas introduced his daughter, Florence. "William here has told me he can repair anything from a carriage to a shotgun."

"How very clever of you, William," said Florence. I did like being called *William,* and not *Willie*—for the moment. Especially when I heard her give the name a saucy spin.

Her face was thin and pale, her eyes green. I had little doubt that I had seen her before—and that she was, in fact, female. She removed her bonnet, shaking down a lock of her long brown hair, perhaps to banish any doubt from my mind. She was striking in appearance, a slight, determined-looking, beautiful young woman.

"No doubt you are faster with your hands," she said, "than you are on your feet."

Nicholas and Blackbeard gave me measuring looks with twinkling eyes, not bothering to disguise their amusement.

Perhaps the sight of my speechless surprise awakened her to something like pity. She added, with a glance at her companions, "Although you could easily outrun any of the other men I know."

This graceful person was, in truth, the thief I had chased through the twilight in Panama City. "I am glad," I managed to say, "to see you in such good spirits."

"Oh, none of my family are ever sick," said Florence, implying that ceaseless good health was a fault. "The entire Barrymore clan can live on fried shoes and boa constrictors."

"Although your dog, from what I understand, suffered some ailment." I was trying to sound urbane, and to prove myself not a complete fool.

"Timothy killed him," said Florence.

Blackbeard nodded, and his features took on a self-conscious glow.

"For barking," added Florence.

"Timothy has the regrettable habit," said Nicholas, "of being quick with his knife."

·❦[CHAPTER 26]❦·

We had been out of San Francisco half an hour, sailing across the bay, heading toward the inland goldfields.

Captain Deerborn was introducing me to the water sloshing in the *Nyad*'s hull. "You notice the bilge is dark and smelly," he said.

"Very," I agreed. Very dark, I meant, and likewise very smelly.

"That's a good sign," he said cheerfully. "It means she's leaking slowly. But it won't last—as soon as she sails against the river, her planks will start to work."

"I see," I said, understanding in part what I was being told.

"They'll work and leak," he continued. "I don't care at all—this is my last voyage on this little ship. I'll tie her up at Sacramento City, and the sturgeon fish can set up housekeeping in the cabin, for all I care."

"You're already rich?" I had to ask.

"Rich?" He chuckled thoughtfully, but he was polite enough to take the question in all seriousness. "No, not entirely within the normal definition of the word. But I do have my prospects."

"Have you staked a claim?" I asked, using a bit of gold-mining jargon I had picked up. Miners joined with companions to file papers, naming a given plot of land theirs to exploit as they wished.

"I was a lawyer's clerk," he replied, "for a shipping company back in Baltimore, but what I really loved was digging and planting."

"You're going to sell seed?"

"Mining essentials," he said, but for the moment gave me no further information, as though he had taken out a patent on a new invention and kept it secret to himself. He did, however, produce a stoneware jug, unstopper it, and offer me a drink of fiery spirits. I accepted it with a show of good manners, eager not to offend my employer.

He leaned close and whispered, "Hardware."

"That sounds very important," I said, still largely mystified.

The captain clapped me on the back. "Shovels, Willie. And picks!"

The captain and I emerged into the fog-filtered daylight to see a stew of passengers, two men locked in combat in their midst. One of them fell as we approached—or slipped on the wooden deck—and people flung themselves out of his way as he scrambled to regain his footing and failed in the damp morning air.

A man with a copper-colored, spade-shaped beard stood with a whip handle—a short, stubby truncheon—in his gloved hand.

Timothy Barrymore crouched on the deck, men crowding away from him. Nicholas emerged from the crowd and helped his family member to his feet. Florence was nearby, peering from behind a stocky passenger, her eyes bright.

"This man stuck an elbow into my side," said the man with the whip handle. "Pushing me like I was a sack of coffee beans." He gestured, demonstrating a quick, painful jab in the ribs. "And so I hit him. And I'll hit him again."

Timothy smiled within his black beard.

⪻ CHAPTER 27 ⪼

This was the sort of raw Western behavior I had once anticipated but, as before, the potential violence was soon dissipated.

"Gentlemen," cried Captain Deerborn in a robust, senatorial tone, staring from one to the other of the two combatants. "I beg your kind attention, if you please."

The captain had the gift of natural authority, unfeigned and easy. Every voice fell silent.

"Gentlemen, if you please," he continued, liquor having perhaps given him a regard for his own speech. "Justice in California is quick, and rarely needed. A killer faces the noose or the garrote, and the thief earns twenty lashes." A garrote was a wire or cord used to throttle the victim from behind. Twenty lashes was scarcely a more merciful punishment—many criminals died from being whipped.

"We find in California," added the captain, "that the best proof against bloodshed is good manners."

"I'm sure my nephew is sorry for any harm," said Nicholas in a firm, gentle voice. The Barrymores had gathered, a silent gang.

Timothy was bleeding from his scalp and gave no sign of being anything but silently amused by the captain's address.

I stepped forward, placing my body between Timothy and the aggrieved passenger.

"I know these people," I said.

What possessed me to protest the harmlessness of this unsavory Barrymore I could not name—perhaps that taste of whiskey. But as I spoke, I looked around at the swarm of faces and caught Florence's eye. She gave me a smile.

And I felt the strangest warmth flood through me.

"And who are you?" asked the red-bearded passenger with heavy emphasis, looking me up and down.

"Willie here is one of the crew," Captain Deerborn replied.

"Oh, well, I guess that makes all the difference," said Redbeard sarcastically.

But perhaps it did. Besides, the passengers were already losing interest, spitting over the side, drawing on their tobacco pipes and cigars. A small group settled back to a game of dominoes; somewhere a deck of cards was being shuffled.

I worked my way over to where Florence was knotting her bonnet, making a ladylike show of making sure it was secure on her head.

"I'm not sure California is prepared," I said, "for an invasion of Barrymores."

"Whatever do you mean?"

"Just making a casual observation," I said, worried that I might have offended her. The truth was that I wanted to talk with her very much, and see her smile at me again.

"I swear to you," she said, "that we are by no means as coarse as you must think us."

Ben would have had some witty rejoinder to this pretty speech, but I could do little more than touch my finger to my hat and pull a twist of tobacco from my pocket. I felt as I did so, that this was not an appropriate offering for a young woman in such a handsome—if slightly worn-looking—headdress.

But she accepted a chew—a good pinch of tobacco disappearing into the shadowy interior of her bonnet.

"My mother passed away last winter," she said. "And we see little reason to stay out of trouble in her absence."

I expressed my sincere condolences. But then I heard myself ask, shocked at my own bluntness, "Is that why you steal from drunken schoolmasters?"

She took a long moment before she spoke again. "Please don't think so poorly of me. I was putting a coin back into that poor man's pocket—it had fallen out, along with some papers and a broken watch fob."

I thought about this. "Why did you run so hard, if

you were innocent?" I asked, unable to disguise my skepticism. But I hated myself at the same time, wishing I could banter with her, like a gentleman of the world, and win yet another smile.

"Because some big brute with a knife strapped to his leg came galloping along—hollering out of his face."

I wondered if I could have mistaken what I had seen in the Panama street.

Galloping. The word stung. I had fancied myself quite a nimble runner. And surely I had not made much noise.

"I swear on my mother's grave," she added, "that I am no thief. Although," she added, "I am not sure most gold seekers are much better than robbers, hurrying like crazy men to dig nuggets out of the ground."

I explained my own particular reasons for coming to California, speaking as plainly as delicacy would allow. I was not just another gold seeker, I told her. My journey would be complete, I told her, if I found Ezra and explained to him why he was required back home.

Florence leaned against the rail, and I joined her, both of us watching an egret as it hesitated, startled by the approach of the schooner.

"And is this Elizabeth back home a special friend of yours?" she inquired.

"A good friend," I agreed. But then I found myself adding, "But not in the way you might mean."

"Is it possible, then, that you did not leave a lady back in Philadelphia?"

"No, you could say, in all fairness, that I didn't." I

was afraid that the truth made me sound plain and unworldly.

Timothy made his way along the rail. I realized that I had never heard the voice of this darkly bearded member of the clan.

The blood was drying to a long bright wrinkle along his cheek. He gave me a conspiratory nod, with the same combination of gentleness and danger displayed by his father, his eyes twinkling but studying me, perhaps wondering if he would have to cut my throat to keep me from barking—or doing anything to harm Florence.

At that moment the white-feathered egret took to the air, circling over the auburn marshland. Timothy made a show of holding an imaginary fowling piece, following the water bird's flight.

Florence stood very close to me.

"William," she said, "the women of Philadelphia must be as dumb as oysters."

I couldn't keep myself from laughing. "Florence, what would make you say such a thing?"

"Because," she said, "you seem to me like a person very well worth knowing."

·❦[CHAPTER 28]❦·

Captain Deerborn gave me a quick verbal sketch of California geography, between sips of fiery corn liquor.

A long inland valley, scored by a few navigable rivers, was skirted by rugged foothills. Beyond the ascending hills, to the east, lofted the mighty Sierra Nevada. It was in the streams and culverts of the mountain foothills that the gold was being found. Word was that soon California would join the United States. Meanwhile, the American government did what it could to deliver mail and defend California waters from theoretical foreign intrusion—British, Russian, Spanish. Nevertheless, as anyone could see, no central government operated with any coherence in this lively land.

"There's a newly situated U.S. courthouse in Monterey," said the captain, "but communications being mostly slow, mining camps deal with felons independently, as the need arises."

"On the field of honor," I suggested.

The captain shook his head emphatically. "If there's a death there's an inquest, Willie, and a sensible trial if one is needed. I saw a legal proceeding in Benecia a couple weeks back, and read about one down in Jamestown. We're gold seekers, not barbarians."

I spent most of the time during our short voyage up the Sacramento River belowdecks. The bilge was no longer so black and foul-smelling—it was running clear through the pumps, a bad sign. I liked my fellow laborers, a cobbler from Albany, a glassblower from Toronto.

It was the second morning upriver.

I was on deck washing down a mouthful of corn bread with thick, sweet coffee, the landscape around the river low and flat. An autumnal mist obscured the horizon, and waterfowl veered up out of the sere marshland. As I looked on, a large golden-furred creature raised up out of the rushes, marsh water streaming from his fur.

The bear watched our passing vessel, his brute presence radiating silence.

At last the effort of standing on his hind legs wearied him, and he lowered his bulk back down again, into the thick autumn-brown vegetation.

The creature continued to graze, in a meditative, cowlike manner.

A few of the Barrymore clan, leaning over the side of the schooner, saw him, too. By their gestures I discerned that they were discussing what firearms they would use to bring down such a bruin.

Florence was among them, and when I approached she came forth to meet me.

"What would you hunt a bear with, Willie?"

"A friend with a wide-bore gun," I answered at once.

She gave me a smile and laughed, and put her hand out to mine.

And kept it there for a good long time.

When I saw Captain Deerborn again, I managed to ask, "Are there many bears in California?"

"Of course there are bears," he said, "both grizzly bears and brown."

He went on to name the genus and species of the large omnivores, and I wondered once again what sort of wild land I was about to encounter, and how I could make Florence a part of my life here.

The captain interrupted his recitation of animal lore when he saw that I was preoccupied. He rested a hand on my shoulder. "The Western bear does not bother visiting a lawyer, it's true," he said. "But the really dangerous creatures out here are all human."

The voyage against the river current was only expected to take two days—three if the wind was utterly contrary—and the labor at the pumps was enjoyable, in a rough sort of way. My fellow pump mates were good-spirited men who swore at the pumps, the smelly water, and the cheap whiskey, but sang about the sun being so hot they froze to death, and other popular tunes. I joined in, even when the liquor made my head ache.

I wanted to have another talk with Florence Barrymore. But I was so hard-worked—and so drunk with whiskey, like every other crew member—that I saw only the slopping water around my feet, and the cheerful features of Captain Deerborn when it was time to swig another dose of spirits.

But the memory of her smile—and the way she had taken my hand—stayed with me.

As we approached the crowd of river vessels along the wharf at Sacramento City, Captain Deerborn led me into his cabin.

He opened an oak chest with a stout iron key, picked out a coin about the size of a shirt button, and placed it in my hand. It was a gold U.S. dollar, and I closed my fist around it thankfully. He cocked his head, and gave me another just like it.

I thanked him sincerely—I was being generously paid for what was, after all, unskilled labor. Passage from San Francisco to Sacramento itself usually cost ten dollars.

"If you can drive a team of horses, William," said the captain, "you've got passage up into the goldfields proper."

I could not hide my eagerness. "I can drive any sort of coach, sir."

After Mr. Ansted had repaired a wagon, I'd drive it out under the chestnut trees, just to make sure the wagon was sound. I knew how to handle reins and carry a whip—no mean accomplishment.

But in my heart I was not sure I was equal to the rugged gold-country roads.

"Are you sure you can handle a six-horse hitch?" he asked. We were both crowded around by crates and dreadfully warm, the iron stove throwing out more heat than we needed.

"Horses or mules, on any sort of road," I insisted, nearly convinced that it was true.

"This will be uphill," he cautioned, "all mire and boulders."

This made me hesitate.

I had once forded a spring-flood creek while delivering a wagon to a drayage company in Frankfort, but I had no experience driving horses over mountains. I had driven well-mannered Philadelphia teams along the roads around town, and I had never had to lash the horses excessively. An experienced carriage man was called a whip—for good reason. To master stubborn, spirited animals, a skilled use of the lash was mandatory, and I was a novice at such driving.

I had barely enough pride and stubbornness to allow myself to add, "I think you'll find me equal to the task, sir."

Captain Deerborn smiled. "I'm very glad, Willie. This is an advance against your wages as a wagon driver." He gave me one more gold coin. "Although I'm close to being a pauper, except for my expectations."

"We won't spend any time at all in Sacramento City?"

"You don't want to spend any time there," he said with a wave of his hand, a man dismissing an utterly disagreeable subject. "That place is a cess-hole, and no place at all for a hardware merchant."

I explained that I was seeking an old companion, and wanted to give him good news.

"You'll find him easily enough," said the captain in his rough but kindly way. "Drop by the New York Hotel, not far from the river. But remember," he added, "be back by noon, or I'll be forced to hire some other whip and be off without you."

·❦[CHAPTER 29]❦·

The dockside was lined with abandoned vessels, schooners and flatboats.

From what we could see of it from the wharf, the entire town had the look of a place that had been set up just the night before.

As we disembarked, a few townsfolk splashed down through the wet encampment to spit tobacco juice and comment cheerfully to one another on the character and dress of the newcomers.

The Barrymore party, their tattered greatcoats and mantles wet with the rain, milled about near the riverbank, while travelers who could afford them hired boys to carry their trunks into town. I tried to catch a further glimpse of Florence, but except for Nicholas, his white hair streaming wet, the group was now an indistinguishable mass of wet folk.

A step pressed the wet earth nearby, and I turned at the sound of my name.

"You will stop by Dutch Bar, won't you, William?" said a woman's voice hopefully.

Florence smiled at me from within a heavy oilcloth hood. I would not have recognized her if she had not spoken.

"You are a mistress of every possible disguise," I remarked with a laugh.

Her green eyes peered into mine—she was not about to be put off with an idle remark.

"Where will I find Dutch Bar?" I heard myself ask. I very much wanted to have greater skill with words—and tell her that parting from her was more than painful.

"Somewhere up the American River," she replied, looking around to see an approaching figure—Timothy, his long dark beard streaming rainwater.

"My uncle Jeremiah has a claim up there," she continued, "and we're set to join him."

Timothy's lips took on the shape of a word, and he took a long time in making a sound. "Come along, Flo," he said, forming the sounds with difficulty, like a man with a crippling stammer.

If Timothy felt any friendship toward me, he disguised the emotion very well.

He kept one hand on Florence's arm, leading her along both protectively and like a guard securing a prize.

But she tossed her arm free and hurried to me.

"William," she said, taking my hand, "I hope we see each other again soon."

Some more artful person would have been able to say something poetic. I could only manage, "Florence, I hope so, too."

She turned back in my direction, and gave me, I thought, a wave of melancholy—or even of longing.

And I stayed right where I was, until her family had led her along and I couldn't see her anymore.

The New York Hotel was a wooden building with a broad front porch, one of a few structures nailed together. Every other shelter was made of canvas—tall tents, broad tents, tents closed up, others open all around.

I spied the hotel long before I could reach it, impeded from my progress by the depth and variety of the ruts in the street. The wheel ruts were mountainous, new and deeper ones being cut, as I watched, by great dray wagons leaving long ridges of stiff mud in their wake. Men trying to cat-foot neatly across the street were soon mired to their boot tops. A single such boot stood alone near the edge of the street, where some exasperated pedestrian had extricated himself and escaped.

"Late from Paris, the renowned opera tenor Lionel Seymour," proclaimed one theatrical advertisement, crowded around by others on adjacent buildings. I knew that Ben was bound to arrive here, with his traveling players—but I no longer felt such a longing to see him.

I was off adventuring on my own, and not doing badly—so far.

Open-sided tents sold mining equipment. A simple wood-shafted hoe cost two dollars, while a cradle and bucket—necessary gold-processing gear—cost twenty-five. If a gold seeker needed a tent of his own, it would cost twelve dollars, and I realized that if I had come to this country to seek my fortune, I would be too poor to even begin.

I was directed to the rear of the hotel, where a building resembling a stable leaned up against the two-story inn. Instead of livestock, the shelter was home to shelves crammed with bales and bundles of envelopes and yellowing newspaper.

"Express companies deliver mail up and down the Sierra," said the clerk, a young man my age but with a manner so nonchalant and knowing that he made me feel like an unlettered savage. "Private companies deliver the mail," he explained. "Sometimes just one or two men with a mule go out with the letters, and sell newspapers from the States at the price of a dollar. The U.S. Post Office disapproves, but nobody listens to bureaucrats around here. There's thousands of pieces of undelivered mail," the clerk concluded, "right here in this annex."

"I'm about to head up to the foothills myself," I said.

"Is that right?" intoned the clerk with a show of the mildest possible interest.

"I could deliver a parcel of letters for you."

He studied me for a moment. "Where are you going?"

I had no idea, and I am afraid my eyes gave away my ignorance. "I'm looking for Ezra Nevin of Philadelphia," I said.

The clerk made no further remark.

I recalled Ben's comment about bribes—it seemed so long ago. I pulled out my three U.S. dollars.

I put one of them down on the counter.

The clerk looked at it with the smallest amount of interest. "I haven't seen an actual minted coin for quite some time."

I waited.

"Ezra who?" he asked after a silence.

I put another dollar there on the counter, beside the first.

"This is a land crammed with Ezras," said the clerk. He leaned forward and confided, "It's a very common name."

I put my third—and last—dollar on the broad oak counter. I would be very short of funds, now, and forced to live on pancakes and water.

He snapped the coins off the shiny countertop and said, without a pause, "I know the man."

I was astonished at this news, and must have given an involuntary jump, because the clerk took a steadying step back away from the counter.

Something about my enthusiasm melted his reserve, and he gave me the hint of a smile. "Well, it's possibly another Ezra with the same surname," he said. "He has a standing order for the Philadelphia *North American*."

"That's him!" I said, trying to restrain my high spirits.

"And what's strange," said the clerk, "is that another man was here looking for him just yesterday. A gentleman with red hair, by the name of Murray. With a couple of rough-looking companions."

⸗⸪[CHAPTER 30]⸪⸗

It seemed like a legend from a distant era—Ezra confronting Samuel Murray on the field of honor in a green meadow outside Philadelphia, the big redhead losing his nerve and hurrying off into the dawn.

But there was a stony logic to it, too: the banking scion stubborn in his humiliation, determined to track Ezra down and win honor at last. I thought of it in those romantic terms, the same ideals that drove men like Murray and Ezra—and, indeed, had until recently compelled me to travel so far from home.

I picked my way along wooden boards arrayed across the muddy street, conflicting responsibilities making me oblivious to the unsteady footing. I wheeled my arms and balanced precariously, and would have fallen into the quagmire if a cheerful man with a Scottish accent had not seized my arm.

"Right you are, there, friend," said the Scotsman, hurrying off across the planks.

Right I am. It was a hopeful turn of phrase, and I liked it.

But I could not bear the thought of Murray finding Ezra—Murray and his two rough companions.

"I wouldn't go near that place," called a voice.

A man in mud-caked boots stalked across the mud, oblivious to the swampy street, already filthy with it. He gestured with the ax he was carrying, using the tool the way a dandy might flourish a silver-knobbed walking stick. "That hellhole," he added, indicating the shadowy site with the ax handle, "is the hospital."

Rows of men lay on cots, attended by shadowy figures. Men were prostrate, mouths agape, and a faint but unmistakable odor of illness drifted out from the confines of the wide, canvas-hooded shelter.

Captain Deerborn was having trouble with a roan horse when I found him, the animal tossing his head and spattering foam all around. The captain was trying to check the animal's bridle, and the horse had taken a particular dislike to him.

"Damn it, Willie, I thought you'd run off," said the captain.

I quieted the animal by making a soft clucking noise. The big roan turned to eye me and shook its head vehemently. My thoughts were in a muddle, and I was grateful to have a practical, immediate problem to attend to.

I pictured all too clearly the jaunty, life-loving form of Ezra Nevin shot through by Samuel Murray, the banker's son.

The image continued to give me little pleasure—far from it.

"This is an angry animal," said Captain Deerborn. "Cunning and resentful."

"I think he's a noble beast," I said hopefully, rubbing the horse between the eyes with my knuckles.

"Noble, possibly, but mad," said the captain. "As many monarchs are."

The big roan was going to be my left-side leader, one of two lead horses in the team of six. The other horses wore blinders and had the stolid, worn-in quality of animals that had hauled freight for many years. Even so, the high spirits of the roan were making them work at their bits and stir from the placid mood most horses fall into when there is nothing much to do.

I climbed up onto the wagon. I perched there high above the ground, and felt the weight of the reins in my hands. I regretted taking on this responsibility, but felt that it was far too late to back down. Furthermore, I didn't want to disappoint the captain.

The mud wagon—the least expensive, sturdiest sort of carriage—was loaded with crates, and a similarly loaded wagon occupied by Captain Deerborn had settled into the wet earth right behind it. Beside me on the high driver's seat was a young man in a flop-brimmed hat who introduced himself as Johnny P. Dorman. He held a crowbar upright, like a weapon, and I gathered that he was there to help if the wheels got stuck between rocks.

Boyish and lean, he looked a good deal younger than I was. I had the beginnings of a beard, and seasons of working with horses and wagon wheels had given me a certain amount of muscle. Johnny was brown-haired and brown-eyed—he admitted to being a full sixteen years old, and it might have been true. Rugged travel and fitful weather made the young and not-so-young all look about the same age.

"Ever drive a team before, Johnny?" I asked. I sounded, to my own ears, rock-ribbed and about forty years old.

"Sure," said Johnny with a studied toss of his head that told me he knew much less about horseflesh than I did.

We both laughed, nervous but instantly liking each other. For the moment we weren't going anywhere. Captain Deerborn went over an inventory, a broad book bound in leather.

"I was up at Dog Bar," Johnny said while we waited for the captain to give the command to move. "But I couldn't find any color, so I came back down to earn the fare home to New Jersey."

Only part of what he had just said—the reference to his home state—made any sense to me. *Color?*

"That's what they call gold in the ground," said Johnny with a touch of pride at his knowledge. "Or glimmering in the bed of a river—*color*, because it's pretty, after all."

Captain Deerborn shut his book. "Hi ho, men!" he sang out, the common idiom for *Let's go!*

I flicked the whip, just once to get the team's respect, and they leaned forward in their traces.

The wagon creaked, but we went nowhere.

Johnny leaped down, his feet squelching in the mud, and put his shoulder into the wagon as I lashed the air with the whip, putting my will into it. The lash gave out a satisfying crack.

This time the wheels lurched, the horses strained, and as Johnny flung himself back beside me we began to roll, the wagon rims huge with mud that began to fly through the air, all over Johnny, all over me.

But we were gaining speed.

❦[CHAPTER 31]❧

For a long while I drove well.

The roan settled into his harness fine once he had a sense of destination, the captain's equally heavily laden wagon rumbling along behind us.

Besides, while the route was new to me, the horses must have known it well, the main road east toward the foothills and gold. The team had that reserved, knowing angle to their ears. Horses may be unintelligent, but I believe they have deep memories.

"You've seen nuggets lying around like that?" I couldn't keep myself from asking after giving the question considerable thought. "In a streambed, glittering?"

"Dog Bar was filthy with the stuff," Johnny said. He was full of gold lore, and he liked to talk. "A bar is an obstruction in a waterway," he added, no doubt aware that he was dealing with a rank newcomer. "Gravel, mostly, or sand. Some of them are riddled with color."

"Fortune did not smile on you?" I asked formally, trying to put the question as inoffensively as I could.

"Well, I got out of there alive," he said thoughtfully. "I count that good fortune enough."

It was hard to converse and handle the horses at the same time, and even harder to absorb the information I had received back at the hotel annex. I had to find Ezra soon.

I prayed that I was not already too late. But we were carried along by a spirited team of horses. With any luck we would arrive well ahead of Murray, who would no doubt have to wait in line for a ticket on one of the slow passenger coaches, try to hire one of the scarce riding horses—or be forced to walk. Most travelers, in fact, made their way on foot, mules carrying their provisions.

"But I know no one is likely to kill me," Johnny was saying. "I had my skull read in San Francisco."

Phrenology was the science—or subtle art—of reading an individual's character and even his future by feeling the irregularities of his cranium.

"Dr. Spence Crawford," Johnny was saying, "studied my head in his office on Market Street. He said I was destined to keep it attached to my neck."

I affect a certain skepticism regarding diviners of all sorts—card readers, water witchers, and even prophetic pigs. But at the same time I do suffer from the human frailty known as envy. As I had envied Ezra his attractiveness to men and women, and Ben his easygoing talent for entertaining an audience, now I envied Johnny his confidence regarding his future.

"Did you pick up any of the art?" I asked.

"The phrenological science? No," said Johnny with a show of polite condescension. "That takes years of study." He must have sensed my momentary disappointment, because he added, not wanting my feelings to be hurt, "Your head looks about like mine. I bet Dr. Crawford would predict neither one of us will be murdered."

On level ground horses trot along prettily enough, the bridle jingling, singletrees attaching the harness to the carriage swinging easily. The reins for the wheelers—the horses closest to the wagon—run between your third and little finger, and it wasn't long before the leather chafed the skin there, rubbing it raw. It requires concentration and strength to drive horses along a road, although the truth is that on a flat or gently rising highway, the horses run easily.

It's anticipation that wearies the driver—watching for deep puddles in the road, or a boulder that has fallen from a nearby bank. Not to mention steadying the horses when a dog decides to hurry along beside, yapping.

But the big roan's character was proving reliable, after all. Clods of mud were flying as the team found a satisfying rhythm, and I kept the whip between the thumb and forefinger of my right hand, the butt secure by the heel of my thumb, like any coachman who knows what he's doing.

My demonstration of driving competence was enough to impress Johnny, who confided in me that his partners had died up at Dog Bar, where no one he knew had found much gold.

"Were they killed?" I had to ask.

"Killed or sick, it doesn't matter," said Johnny, sadly.

It did matter to me. If California was a land where old scores were beginning to be settled violently—as I now suspected—I wanted to know.

But I let the matter rest, and at last Johnny offered, "The chairman of our gold mining enterprise dropped dead from overwork. The bylaws made our vice-chairman head of our enterprise, but he got sick, and my friend broke his leg, and it swelled up and killed him. The lawyer among us, who wrote up all our paperwork, got pneumonia. Those of us who didn't die quit for home."

"Except for you," I said.

Johnny shook his head, implying that he himself did not count for much.

"But I know an Irishman," said Johnny, stirring himself to better spirits, "who has dry diggings up-current, past Spanish Bar. He worked ten thousand dollars out of the quartz rock."

"Where is Spanish Bar?" I asked.

"Oh, you don't want to go there," said Johnny. "There's no use—it's all staked, the claim filed, I heard. It's worked by a couple of gentlemen miners, a man named Andrew Foll-something and his friend Ezra Nevy."

"Nevin," I corrected.

As I explained that one of the well-spoken men was a former associate of mine, the already increasing respect I had earned from Johnny flowered into full admiration.

"Those two dandies," he said, "have had one lucky strike after another!"

The wagon rolled along sweetly, each horse trotting without a care. I wished Ben could see me then—or Florence.

When we reached the foothills my troubles began.

·◦⟨ CHAPTER 32 ⟩◦·

This was a countryside of oak trees and rocky outcrop-
pings, hills and dry fields. Newspapers had praised the
nugget-rich streams and the harvest-swollen vineyards,
neither of which I had actually set eyes upon yet. But no
journalist had expressed the naked reality I saw all
around me. The land possessed a sweet wildness, and a
rolling, far-off horizon that quickened the heart.

The horses labored up the low hills successfully,
leaning forward in their harnesses, needing no more
than a quiet click of my tongue and a gentle twitch of
the multitudinous reins to remind them of their duty.

From the low summits of these ridges we could see
distant mountains, dark peaks splashed with snow.
They were more grand than any range of highland I
had ever seen, and they stirred me to realize that I was

in the midst of a great adventure, close to both wildness and riches.

I began to pen a letter to Elizabeth in my mind. In this imaginary epistle I offered the opinion that the men of the Golden West were rough, but confident; plainly dressed, but filled with a sense of purpose. Such phrases pleased me, well balanced and thoroughly reasoned—the prose of a worldly man. I looked forward to dipping a quill into an inkwell, and putting these thoughts on paper.

We began to go downslope from time to time. We would clop along to the modest crest of a hill, and then rattle downward, splashing through another shallow creek in the bosom of the hills. Even this change in topography did not alarm me, lost in my own thoughts.

But then we passed a wagon that had suffered a mishap, crates and mining equipment strewn all over the shoulder of the road. One of the stricken horses lay on its side, flanks heaving, still tangled in its harness. The faces of the passengers and driver were masks of anguish and frustration.

The wagon had gathered too much momentum on its way down a hill, and overrun its team—a well-known danger of such roads, and one my experience in no way equipped me to confront.

Captain Deerborn's inquiry carried through the early-afternoon sunlight from behind us, his voice asking if the disordered travelers needed any help.

"We'll be back in business in no time," called the

driver, an expert whip, by the look of him—blue trousers thrust into high calfskin boots, a broad-brimmed hat on his head. If such a prime hand had trouble with a wagon, I reasoned, I was in for a difficult afternoon.

Horses get ideas from other horses.

They don't talk to each other, it's true, but you don't want a horse to see a fellow creature in distress, or angry or sulky. The mood catches on, and my team had been close enough to the accident so that even the ones wearing blinders could peer around and get the general idea of equine catastrophe.

The roan began to pull to the left, right out in front of the occasional oncoming wagon. I had the leader reins between my fore and middle fingers, and drew on them enough to guide the horse back in line, but he turned one ear around as though to catch what I was telling Johnny.

"That big roan," I was saying, "wants to dump us in the road."

Just then we passed a squashed snake in the road, the worst thing a horse can see, aside from a snake that happens to be alive.

You hope horses aren't paying attention when they trot past a specimen like that. And none of the horses did see it, except Roan, and he shied badly, trotting stiffly, lifting his nose. A ridge of hair rose up along his spine.

I cluck-clucked and kept pressure on the reins, and soon we began to labor up a long hill. Johnny leaped down, and put a shoulder to the wagon. Even his little bit of strength helped, the horses sweating and beginning to breathe hard.

But when we came to the top of the hill, the long, wheel-rutted road swept down before us. The animals were breathing even more heavily as we crested the summit, and kept their even pace with effort as they met the downslope.

In no time at all we were going too fast, leaving Johnny far behind. The heavy wagon, creaking and rattling, began to gain momentum, pushing the horses ahead of its gradually accelerating mass.

My teeth rattled, every bone in my body shaken hard. Drivers had been known to be flung from a wagon as it barreled over a rough road. I tried to remember, without looking, where the brake happened to be.

Some wagons have a brake handle you pull on and pray, and others have a brake pedal worked by foot. This wagon had a well-worn pedal, I discovered at last, and I put my foot out for it and missed, the wagon rocking too hard. When I finally got my boot on the brake pedal, I stepped on it with my full weight.

It's important to take the slack out of the reins just before you apply the brake, and the horses usually put their ears back, anticipating by the sound of your boot settling on the pedal what you are about to do.

The horses slowed their pace—or tried to. The wheels gave a squeal.

The wagon did not slow down. I used my full strength,

and depressed the pedal all the way, standing on it with every ounce of effort. The brakes smoked, friction against the wheel making them hot.

We were slowing down—that much was true. But if anything, we were losing speed far too quickly. Captain Deerborn's wagon rattled along behind, growing closer with each heartbeat.

I hauled on the reins, too hard at first, trying to guide the wagon to the edge of the road. The roan began to skirmish with his fellow horses, confused or annoyed. At the same time I made the low, gentle noise drivers make, a sound spelled *whoa,* but in truth a nearly mournful and strangely soothing syllable.

Johnny caught up with the wagon at the bottom of the hill. I was careful to give no clue, sitting there with the whip cocked in my fist, that—until moments before—I had been terrified.

"Good driving," panted Johnny.

I nodded, trying to appear in command. I was thankful to be alive.

"Are you all right, Willie?" called Captain Deerborn. I gave a wave with my whip, and the mere shadow of the lash caused the horses to start forward.

"Up ahead a good way is Putah Slough," said Johnny, when he had caught his breath. "That is the really dangerous part of the trip."

·⊰ Chapter 33 ⊱·

My body was sore, every sinew and every bone, and the reins had cut into my hands.

But we were safe, and the horses, sweating and laboring, were unhurt.

"*Putah* is a Spanish word for 'whore,'" Johnny was reporting confidingly, pronouncing it *hoor.* "Sometimes a bandit waylays a wagon here," he added, with the air of someone with privileged knowledge. "And shoots every passenger."

"That's a lot of trouble," I said, trying to give the impression that those tidings did not bother me a bit. In a way, I would have welcomed a robber as a bit of variety at that point. "Wasteful of time and powder—why doesn't he just chop them up with an ax?"

"There they are!" said Johnny.

I was in a virtual trance just then, late-afternoon shadows flowing over the team of horses. I was beyond weariness, beyond aching joints and matter-of-fact terror, and nearly—very nearly—enjoying myself.

"Bandits!" said Johnny excitedly, with an air of satisfaction, perhaps eager to see what an expert whip like his new companion would do.

California had been populated by a graceful, Spanish-speaking people before the rush for gold—cattle ranchers and horse breeders. This scattered population had been overwhelmed by the burgeoning hordes of Americans, but here and there you could see evidence of their way of life: a darkly mustached individual on a glossy, spirited horse, or a dark-eyed woman under a shawl.

Or in this instance a trio of adventurers in sombreros, making no secret of their presence, pistols thrust into their belts. They looked every inch like stage actors set forth to represent romantic brigands.

The tallest of the three raised a hand, and I hauled on the reins, the team coming to a halt accompanied by a creak and rattle from every joint in the carriage frame.

"Don't dally with those lawless vagrants, Willie," called out Captain Deerborn from far behind.

The leader said something to me in Spanish, and stepped to the side of the carriage, trying to inventory our stock through the well-lashed canvas tarpaulin.

"What do you have, my friend?" he asked in heavily accented English.

"Mining tools," I said, as noncommittally as possible.

I had to admire the sashes around their waists, and the silver buttons on their shirts. For some reason the three dashing men made me only the least bit uneasy, perhaps because I had used up all the terror in my constitution earlier that day.

The tall Californian slapped a hand against the tarpaulin, and the cargo gave a muted iron chime.

Captain Deerborn was breathing heavily, hurrying up on foot, protesting, "No, you aren't stealing any of my shovels."

The tall man turned to one of his companions, and, after a moment's consultation, produced a pair of spurs. He ran his fingers over the rowel of one of the implements, spinning it, and said something in Spanish that meant, by all indications, that he would trade this set of spurs for a Yankee shovel.

The spurs did not gleam, and the leather fastenings appeared toughened by use. Nevertheless, the objects spoke of another world—of stallions and ballads, a finer, almost noble existence compared with our mercantile, Yankee manner of dress and speech.

Captain Deerborn's shoulders slumped with regret, one hand half lifted in temptation.

"Gentlemen," he said, "I'll never have any use for anything so horsemanlike."

Maybe Johnny made a sigh—or maybe it was me.
Captain Deerborn gave us a glance.

"Well," he said, after a long moment. "Well, my friend," he added with a smile, "if it keeps you and your fellows from carving us up."

···✦[CHAPTER 34]✦···

Three days later Johnny and I climbed a rocky trail beside the American River.

Johnny was proving a lively companion, and while I missed Ben's knowledge and enthusiasm, California was a place where old friends were replaced by new ones and the past was at times hard to remember.

The rapids, when I stepped in them, were cold, my feet numb inside my boots. Every gold seeker we passed worked frantically. The water was already high, the first rains of the wet season having lashed the hills. Soon the river would run hard and cold, frustrating nearly every system of separating gold from dross.

The two of us traveled a dirt road strewn with carpetbags, coffee mills, lap desks, saddles, and an assortment of other debris, including fowling pieces and lamps, signs that the last vestiges of refinement were being abandoned as men wearied with the uphill climb. Johnny carried as much as I did, each of us laden with blankets and a small amount of dry corn bread and jerked meat—we had speculated whether the flesh had belonged to a cow, a horse, or a wizened hunting dog.

We had left Captain Deerborn beside a huge mining camp, a city of auburn mud and similarly colored tents, stained from bottom to top with wet. He was hawking his hardware in his stentorian voice, and a long assembly of customers was lining up—whether to make a purchase or to be entertained by the captain's ringing oratory on the quality of his wares, it was difficult to say.

While newspapers in the East had extolled the opportunities for individual enterprise, every mining camp we passed was an example of cooperative effort, one volunteer frying bacon while his mates shoveled sand and gravel into a cradle. These cradles were the most common mining device. Also called rockers, all such contraptions involved shoveling gravel into a hopper, a rough sieve where shaking and stirring allowed the finer grit to fall below, into a long wooden trough.

Water was poured or directed from a stream over these assorted minerals. A long canvas belt allowed the lighter quartz and granite to flow out the open end of the trough, catching the heavy gold-bearing pebbles in the rockers' wooden ribs. Other mining endeavors involved straightforward panning for the treasure—a simple but surprisingly effective system, swilling water and dark sand around and around, until all that was left in the tin pan was the precious element. One burly Welshman we encountered employed the even simpler method, straining black sand through a woolen blanket. He had, according to Johnny's admiring reports, a strongbox crammed with pay dirt.

Johnny continued to be eager to prove his knowledge, and it was very much in the Gold Rush spirit of cooperation that he and I traveled together. At night the sounds of singing echoed down the ravines, and men entertained themselves with fiddles and other musical instruments, while companions played at dominoes or cards. Many camps had posted the names of their outfits, Elmira Mining Enterprise or Bangor Mining Company, along with the names of the presidents or treasurers of the small but booming corporations, and perhaps a copy of their weather-stained bylaws.

"Spanish Bar is still uphill a day or two," Johnny would say, and he seemed to know his way. He predicted that soon we would come upon a camp of Chinese, and sure enough we did, rounding a corner and finding a crew of Asian laboring men, overseen by one of their countrymen. He gave us a wave, but said not a word.

We greeted a camp of Chileans, and another of Swedes, each group identified by Johnny, who prided himself in knowing which camp had a few scarce women and children, and such arcana as which camp had succeeded in killing a wildcat, and where a nugget "the size and shape of a roast potato" had been found under a log.

Even the food arrived from unfamiliar places. Potatoes and coffee hailed from the Sandwich Islands across the Pacific, as did nearly every other vegetable we saw, down to the wrinkled, time-wasted beets one miner was slicing into his frying pan. Sandwich Islanders had joined the other throngs of seekers from around the world, brown-skinned, portly men wrapped in blankets against the unfamiliar chill.

Gold camps had hasty, piratical names: Gouge Eye, Sucker Flat, Red Dog, and You Bet. Most companies were called nothing at all, and the ones we passed by were too preoccupied with pick and shovel, bucket and cradle, to give us much more than a casual glance. We met brief smiles and hurried greetings. Sometimes I took a moment to ask about a red-haired man named Murray and his two companions.

"Red-haired Murray," a miner would say, running the name and description quickly through his mind. "I doubt it," he would offer at last, or "I don't think so," as though a definite *no* was somehow impolite. Offhand courtesy was another characteristic of the Forty-niners. Outright unfriendliness was too much trouble.

And so, apparently, was real violence. Men argued, and swung the occasional fist, but as I had already observed, altercations soon lost their importance. Johnny had exaggerated the threat from bandits. A few high-waymen were rumored to have waylaid shipments of gold near a town on Deer Creek named Rough and Ready, but robbery was uncommon—as were homicide, assault, and most other crimes except public drunkenness. Everyone was too busy to bicker for any length of time, and even chronic drunkards labored blearily beside their sober brethren, shoveling ore.

But men were injured along the river, and there was little doubt that they could be killed. A Frenchman named DuClou sported a slowly healing gash in his forehead—an ax head had flown off its shaft, and nearly taken his life. Other people had nearly drowned crossing the ever-rising river on makeshift bridges, ropes suspended across the current and traversed hand-over-hand.

A Norwegian miner had lost his grip near Welsh Flat the week before, and vanished.

As we approached one shadowy camp that chilly afternoon, Johnny fell silent and looked pointedly away from the lone miner who worked that claim, a tall individual with a shiny bald head.

This solitary man looked vaguely familiar to me, as he stooped to gather up a large firearm.

"This is Dutch Bar," said Johnny in a guarded voice.

"And who's that?" I asked.

"That's Jeremiah Barrymore," said Johnny, in a low voice barely audible over the sound of the tumbling rapids nearby.

My heart leaped at the sound of this familiar name.

"He works all alone," Johnny continued. "Folks

expect that he'll shoot whoever trespasses on his claim."

"How much farther to Spanish Bar?" I asked, light-heartedly considering my chances against a murderous Barrymore.

"We'll be there if we keep going," said my companion. "But," he added with a strained truthfulness, "it's still a good long way."

"How far?" I insisted.

His gaze dropped. "I think we could get there by midnight."

"If we were owls, and could fly, you mean."

The surly-looking man with the bald head surely did not resemble any of the other busy but cheerful miners we had passed. But the sound of his surname stirred friendly feeling in me—and more than a little curiosity. Besides, I was tired, and had long since begun to associate the Barrymores with a variety of flinty friendliness.

"William, don't go up there," cried Johnny.

I made my way up the rocky slope.

·⊰[CHAPTER 35]⊱·

One of the principal arts of shooting is to measure the distance correctly before you pull the trigger.

Jeremiah's eyes played over me as I approached.

I made myself an easy target, walking up to him like that, but Jeremiah had the good manners to keep the double-barreled gun pointed in the general direction of the pine needles on the ground.

The shotgun is the only reliable firearm, in my view, scattering so many pellets that at least part of the target is likely to be hit. The forefinger on Jeremiah's left hand was bound with a yellow bandage, but his trigger finger looked healthy. Smoke from a heap of half-consumed firewood rose up around us, and stung my eyes.

I introduced myself, and I introduced Johnny, too—he crept along behind me despite his warning.

Jeremiah said nothing, and settled one foot ahead of him, like a man getting ready to throw his gun to his shoulder.

"I met up with members of your family in Panama City," I said.

If anything, this news brought a frown to his features, one eyebrow tightening and his lips pressing into a thin line.

"Nicholas and Timothy," I said, hoping the names would act like charms. "And Florence."

Saying her name made me miss her suddenly—a sharp feeling of longing that surprised me. Whatever her character, she was a young woman full of the unexpected. Elizabeth back home was lovely and peaceful—but in my years of drinking tea with her, she had almost never surprised me.

Jeremiah's eyes did seem to soften just a little at word of his relations.

"I took their leave in Sacramento City," I added.

"Are they all right?" he asked in a hopeful voice, setting the butt of his scattergun on the ground.

Jeremiah told us he had some coffee in the pot, and this time I accepted a Barrymore offer of such refreshment without delay. My feet were cold and sore, and I had not had a taste of the beverage for so long I had a stab of the keenest nostalgia, recalling my aunt putting honey into a bright blue cup.

The gold camps I'd passed generally used the same

campfire methods, lighting a fire in the predawn and keeping it going against the autumn chill, a black coffeepot dangling over the coals. Jeremiah's coffee had been cooking all day, and it was thick and bitter. He stirred some brown sugar into it with a stick, and I drank the thick syrup down. I could have sworn that it was the best beverage I had ever tasted.

Johnny was quiet in our host's presence; this was the longest silence I had experienced from my companion in two or three days.

"I crushed my finger," said Jeremiah, in a voice without self-pity.

I expressed sympathy, and he shrugged.

"Your family should be here very soon," I said.

"I welcome the news," he responded, and I realized that Jeremiah had spent so much time in solitude that his conversational powers had rusted over.

"You work Dutch Bar alone?" I asked.

"The Indians quit."

Some miners, I had heard, hired Indians to work the diggings, generally members of the Miwok or Ohlone tribes. Pay disputes arose when miners tried to pay the locals in glass necklaces and fake pearls.

"Solitude can be a hardship," I ventured.

Jeremiah surprised me with a gentle smile. "I grow a little used to it," he said. "But I think our natural condition is to have human company, and plenty of it."

Jeremiah had a pig of lead beside the mound of embers—a large brick of the soft metal. He had been working in the shelter of an outcropping, springwater splashing down the granite escarpment. He had been about to make bullets—buckshot, judging from the mold sitting on the damp earth.

"If you don't mind me making an observation," I said, "your shot mold is wet."

If you pour molten lead into a wet mold, the hot metal will sputter and splash dangerously.

"You try making do with one hand," said our host, with just a trace of testiness. "It isn't easy."

I said that I would make him some buckshot, if he would let us bed down near his fire and share just a little of his corn bread. It was the sort of cordial barter that typified the gold country, and Jeremiah saw the fairness of it.

As we gazed into the campfire, sparks ascending into the mountain dark, I asked if he had seen a red-haired gentleman and a couple of companions heading upriver recently.

Jeremiah was cooking our evening meal. The corn bread was frying in a big black skillet, an operation that took some concentration. Bacon sizzled as he turned it over with a stick. Real bacon was prized by gold diggers—even the most leathery rind of ham flavored the bread fried alongside it, and gave a delicious savor to the smoke. The remnants of preserved meat Johnny and I had been chewing on recently had been rank, and tough as razor strops.

I assumed Jeremiah had not heard me, and I was about to ask again, when he responded, "How can I tell a gentleman from a working man, up here?"

"By their boots," said Johnny, one of the first statements he had made since we had arrived at this camp. "And their guns."

"Is that right?" said Jeremiah dryly.

"Gentlemen have calfskin boots, and English pistols," said Johnny. "And when they talk they say, 'I have to admit' and 'I'm of the opinion.'"

Jeremiah and I laughed at the accuracy of Johnny's observation.

Johnny went into the briefest of sulks.

Jeremiah said, "I have to admit I watch every man who passes this camp. I don't recollect any three travelers like that."

The bacon was delicious, and the fried corn bread, too, our supper washed down with a little whiskey mixed with American River water. Jupiter and Minerva on their thrones did not dine any better.

I shared a taste of the Dutch gin from the flask in my breast pocket, introducing it to Jeremiah as proof against fever. It was a good thing the tonic was good for our health—it tasted bad, and as a result there was plenty left in the container even now.

I was weary enough to sleep well, a mindless, deep slumber that ended abruptly.

A step woke me.

As I watched, Jeremiah knelt by the fire, gazing down toward the river. He wore a blanket like a cloak, the glowing coals illuminating his profile.

I asked him what he had heard.

"What business do you have," he asked, "with three men traveling upriver?"

"What did you see?" I asked.

Gold miners often used language to forestall communication as well as give it. If you asked how successful a man's claim was, he might offer a friendly but vague remark: "Not too bad" or "Could be worse."

Jeremiah was no different. "It's hard to say."

"Did you see them?" I insisted.

Jeremiah considered. "I think I did. Making slow progress along the river trail in the dark."

I peered downslope, all the way down to the white water of the river, a source of reflected starlight.

"Who are they?" he asked.

·⊰[CHAPTER 36]⊱·

Jeremiah offered us some of his very hot coffee well
before dawn, thickened as before with brown sugar.
Johnny and I swallowed gratefully, although the stuff
was nearly too hot to consume.

I was shivering, and stiff from lying on the ground,
and I felt eager to hurry upriver to Spanish Bar. At the
same time I wanted to stay where I was, in the crackling
warmth of Jeremiah's campfire. I was finding Jeremiah
a good companion—steady, alert, measuring out his
words.

He searched in the tent, and brought out a coarse
horsehide sheath. He gave it to Johnny, who accepted
the gift with wide eyes.

"Take her out and heft her," said Jeremiah.

A brilliant Bowie knife gleamed in the faint early
light.

"I can't keep it," protested Johnny.

"Then bring her back," said Jeremiah cheerfully, "when you're done with her."

This puzzled Johnny. "When will that be?" he asked.

Jeremiah smiled, but his eyes were quiet—even somber.

Jeremiah said it was only three miles to Spanish Bar, "but hard going in the rocks, unless you're a goat."

A mist had risen over the river in the early-morning hours, a shadowy river of fog that filled the mountain canyons on either side. Small birds with flashing white tail feathers darted among the red branches of the underbrush. Jays fluttered and squalled in the tall, mist-shrouded pines. It wasn't the first time I realized how sharp-edged and rough the ridges and vegetation of this land were, compared with the dales and barrens of the East.

Johnny swaggered along beside me, his hand going to the hilt of our recent acquisition, drawing it experimentally. It was still dark in the shadows of the huge boulders along the river.

"That's quite a knife," I said, wanting to tell my young companion, without alarming him, that he should appreciate the quality, weight, and beauty of his unexpected possession.

I reasoned that he might need it soon.

⊰[CHAPTER 37]⊱

It was full morning when we arrived. The shadows were still cold, but the sun was hard off the stones, and glittered off the rills of white water.

Spanish Bar was a long spit of black sand, jutting out into the current. The river made a constant, low rumble, coursing over boulders.

One long tent, flaps wide open to the river, glowed in the brilliant daylight. But some more-or-less permanent structures had been erected, too, shacks and lean-tos of white pine timbers. An arm of the river had been diverted by an improvised dam of gravel. The earth all around was so pitted and delved that any hasty progress across it would risk injury.

I crouched beside the river trail and eyed the camp. I had promised myself I would confront Ezra with my news before I uttered a word of greeting. I had dreamed of accusing him of betraying Elizabeth, uttering false promises, and leaving her to be scandalized by her condition.

But at this last moment I was grateful to have made it to this place safely, hopeful that I could preserve Ezra's life.

Johnny made a tiny whisper of impatience through his teeth. "Go on up, Willie," he urged me, "and let them know you're here."

I thought of a dozen greetings, and imagined lifting a full-voiced call over the sound of the river.

To my surprise, Johnny gave a whistle. This was a sharp, keen sound, heart-stopping so close. Even a deaf man would hear such a shrill, piercing sound.

Johnny lowered his gaze in apology, but I nudged him. "Try it again."

No one moved from within a tent. Only the faintest thread of smoke lifted from the fire, where a black kettle hung over half-charred wood. This late in the morning, work should be under way, pick hammers flashing.

"*Ezra!*"

It was my voice, adding to the intermittent shrill of Johnny's whistling. I willed my imagination into hearing his response as I stood and took a tentative step forward.

Willie Dwinelle, is that you?

I wanted to hear the words so badly. Every man's speech got honed down out here in California, fancy talk giving way to a masculine flatness of tone and phrasing. But we were a sentimental lot, too, and old friends shouted greetings and wept with joy, hugging each other after long absence, and every night we had heard singing in the distance, romantic songs about long-lost loves.

Ezra and I would throw our arms around each other. I blinked tears of relief and anticipatory joy at the thought of seeing him, newly bearded and sun-tanned but decidedly his usual, jaunty self, stepping out from the tent right ahead of me. Of course I could not raise a fist against the fellow, and of course he would be the Ezra Nevin I had always known him to be in the old days—a gentleman.

Johnny followed, our boots crunching across the dug-up gravel. I was brimming over with my tidings: Elizabeth expecting a baby, Ezra needed back home, honor requiring him to return at once.

God, it would be good to see him. I wished Ben could be here, too, so we could all trade laughing tales of travel and adventure.

I stopped still. I put out a hand and stopped Johnny in his tracks.

"Wait here," I said.

"What's wrong?" asked Johnny.

But he stayed where he was, frozen by the tone of my voice.

I went forward to the tent, and looked in. I straightened at once.

———&c&c———

I considered what I had just seen.

"William, what is it?" asked Johnny in a voice nearly lost in the roar of the river. I read his eyes, touched with fear, and put my hand out.

Wait.

While I steeled my will to look again at what I had seen, telling myself that I had to be mistaken.

⊰{ CHAPTER 38 }⊱

The interior of the tent had been torn up.

A portable writing desk had been wrenched open, journal pages—dates and neat, brown-inked entries—ripped and scattered. A telescope had been thrown out of its black leather case, and thick canvas miner's trousers sprawled all over the bedding. A one-ounce gold scale lay beside a smashed strongbox, a few scant grains gleaming where treasure had spilled—and someone had scooped most of it up.

Whoever had done this, I reasoned when I could think at all, was not only a killer. He was also a thief.

As though that distinction mattered. I had seen the red splatter, all over the place, but deliberately did not look directly at the source. I put that event off for a few heartbeats. Blood was everywhere, I had observed that much. It was up along the sides of the tent, along with bits of hair, and something else—dark matter. It was all fresh, flies just now discovering the gore.

I could not wait any longer.

I forced myself. I looked, and glanced away immediately. A man lay arms every-which-way, legs sprawled out, his features largely obliterated. I felt some inner resolve leave me and I made myself look yet again.

I left the tent and made my way to Johnny.

Suddenly I hated the up-and-down terrain of this landscape. *Goldfields* had conjured a vision of pastoral fortune hunting, low hills and sparkling nuggets. This campsite was narrow, like so many others, surrounded on three sides by steep, forested mountainside. Unseen eyes could be studying us, even now.

"I want you to head on back to Jeremiah Barrymore," I said. I had to stop then and steady my voice.

"What is it?" asked Johnny.

I tried to prevent him, but he rushed forward, stooped and looked inside.

He was breathing hard, too, when he stood upright again, stiff and hearing me without responding.

"Run back," I told him, "and get Jeremiah."

He didn't move.

"Tell him to bring his shotgun," I continued, "and all the buckshot he can carry."

Johnny stayed right where he was.

I deeply regretted bringing him here, so close to danger.

He shook his head: *Wait.*

I understood Johnny's need to observe it again, bending low to confirm what he had seen.

"Go on, Johnny," I urged him.

"Who is that?" he asked.

I was trembling. It didn't seem that human speech could be possible at such a time. I said, "I believe it's Andrew Follette. Ezra Nevin's friend."

I had scarcely known him. He'd been a young man fond of French cordials and well-bred hunting dogs, I had heard—the perfect companion for Ezra.

"Whoever did this will get me, too," Johnny said when he could speak again. He looked years younger suddenly, a pale and unsteady child.

"The killers don't want to hurt you," I said, in a voice hearty with false confidence. I wanted Johnny away from that camp, safely downriver.

"They'll run me down," he said.

I put my two hands on his shoulders, looking him straight in the eye. "Then you better be fast."

·◄[CHAPTER 39]►·

Johnny fled downriver, and I wondered if I should have left with him. I was afraid of what else I might discover in the camp.

It did not take long. I spied what looked like a pair of trousers tossed down, by the edge of the claim. As I approached I had to stop and check my knife in its scabbard. I took one step, and then another, aware as I drew near that I was closing in on a human body, arms flung, face turned away like a man receiving a slap.

He lay flat on the ground, eyes half open. I had heard that dead people resemble sleepers. He didn't. I felt that I had to touch the corpse, to let him know, in some irrational way, that someone with good sense had found him. His hand was not warm, but it was not cold, either. It was wrapped around a miner's pick, a tool with a sharp spike at one end of its iron head and a flat, hoelike blade on the other. The spike was bloody.

One side of his face was lathered with still-drying soap. This attracted my eye only after I had caught a glimpse of the ugly rent in his clothing, something I did not want to examine right away. I took a breath, steadied my nerve, and took it all in.

In the breast of his well-knit, fawn yellow waistcoat was a dark hole, perfectly round. The bullet hole was seared all around, the woolen fibers black and frizzled. I stood over the young gentleman—the man Elizabeth had loved—and I wept.

The top of his head was gone, the skin of his forehead seared, a round hole just below the hairline. The pistol barrel had pressed against his head—the killer had taken extra care to make sure Ezra was dead. I was furious with myself. If only I had pushed on through the night, and had not lingered by Jeremiah's cheering fire, digesting a belly full of bacon. Even as Johnny and I sat savoring morning coffee, Ezra had lost his life.

Now falling stones whispered, shards and splinters of quartz-rich rock tumbling down from above. I blotted my tears on my sleeve and headed upward, through the boulders. A woodpecker squalled, hiding higher in the sweeping pine branches, and the perfume of woodland surrounded me.

I scrambled, climbing higher up the ridge, the sharp pink-white gravel cutting my fingers, following a trail of blood.

···⊰{ CHAPTER 40 }⊱···

Never before in my life had I felt such fear of solitude.

The days of my boyhood, classrooms and Sunday church, were more remote to me now than the stories of Noah and his Ark and Moses and the Burning Bush. I had always liked my neighbors and my friends, but now I felt a stab of need—a sharp, inner longing for the company of good-hearted people.

This was rank wilderness. No painter in oils or watercolor would ever be able to depict such a woodland—there was nothing pretty about it. But there was something rough and breathtaking about the landscape, a quality beyond poetry. Pines with red-scaled bark speared upward, and sharp-crusted lichen cloaked the rocks. If only I had lingered there with a few companions, I would have considered the vista beautiful.

Somebody just ahead of me had left a trail of blood,

drops of darkening scarlet in the coarse-grained soil.

But I caught no sight of my quarry, the brush ahead quiet and unstirred in the warm, late-morning sun. And the bleeding was slowing down, and ceasing altogether, judging by the smaller and more subtle evidence on the pine needles as I clambered over a ridge, and looked down on a mountainous scene.

Elizabeth used to recite poems, fine verses by Keats and Shelley, and I had once imagined myself cresting peaks in far-off continents, an exploring adventurer like stout Cortez. Now I continued to wish I could be far from this rugged wasteland, right in the middle of some slow and smoky town.

At that moment I saw one of them.

He was curled into a ball at the foot of a moss-cloaked tree, and at first I was certain he was dead.

But at the sound of my step he tried to raise up into a sitting position. All anger left me for the moment, seeing a fellow creature so badly hurt. I reached for the flask at my breast, thinking that I would offer him a sip of juniper spirits, but he produced a knife and made an effort to climb to his feet.

"They're after you, Murray!" he called out.

He sank down again and then, like a dog too weary to do more than curl up, he fell to his side.

When I knelt to help him, he said, weakly, "Don't!"

I reassured the injured man that I would not hurt him. He said again, faintly, "No, damn you."

At last I realized that he meant: Don't touch me. *Leave me alone.*

When I glanced back at him, he had taken on an awkward stillness I could not mistake for life.

I tried to climb upward. The mountain was composed of crumbling granite, crisscrossed by strata of hard, glittering quartz. In places the weathered, mealy granite bits were held together by the black roots of pines, and I clung to these roots as I climbed upward, my fingertips raw.

When I began to slip downward it was a matter of simple inertia, my weight dragging me. But soon there was a small avalanche cascading down, grains of granite down my shirtfront, and when I tried to seize a root, it slipped free of my grasp. On my helpless way down I passed the body, with its look of rapt astonishment, and I wished for my sake that his last words had not been a curse.

I did, in truth, feel close to being damned. With the logic of an event that had happened long ago, I felt my boots shoot out over nothingness, and my body fold around the hard edge of a precipice.

All around me a fan of tumbling stone, skittering down and past me. I could not brake my momentum—I was falling, too, over the root-slashed ledge.

Into empty space.

·◄[CHAPTER 41]►·

I scrabbled, clawing at the rocky surface and the embedded pine roots. I hung on.

But I knew that if I moved again, or even took a deep breath, I would plummet.

I flung one leg up over the granite precipice, the stone warm with morning sunlight, and said, out loud, "That's enough."

I can stay like this forever.

I gathered my strength, trying to meditate on the sparkling granite and the red, searching figures of the ants just a few inches from where I clung. When I felt steady and determined, I extended my hand, feeling for invisible cracks and imperfections that would support me. To my surprise, I breathed no pious prayer during that long moment, nor did I envision the gentle eyes of Elizabeth back home. No grand hymn echoed in my breast.

I thought of Florence.

I held on to a sweeping, fragrant pine bough, and rolled my glance back at the abyss I had just escaped. The void was much shallower than I had sensed, but still enough to break bones, a slope of granite shingle that flowed all the way to the mining claim with its tent and improvised wooden shacks.

I had held on, and I had survived. A sensation of shaky relief, and even triumph, swept me. And the sight of the camp inspired a moment of reverie, the small improvised buildings, nailed upright with the bark still on the lumber. They were like the make-believe dwellings a child might assemble on a rainy day, out of splinters and toothpicks, safe and imaginary—except for the crumpled figure of Ezra Nevin, just visible among the stones.

I was more careful, now, clinging hard to roots, embracing trees, gauging each toehold. A late-season wasp settled down over the remains of the unhappy man as I passed him again, the insect perhaps mistaking blood for blossoms.

I paused once to empty sand and pea-gravel out of my boots. I was just beginning to feel like my normal self, and wished I had a plug of apple-cured tobacco to chew. I labored hard, and as quickly as I was able, and at last stood on a ridge. And immediately fell to one knee behind a tangle of brush.

Just ahead of me sat Samuel Murray.

He was a haggard, whiskery copy of himself, garbed in a thick, loose-fitting coat, his red hair uncombed.

He knelt on a rocky ridge well ahead, in a sandy clearing, pouring powder from a flask into a pistol barrel. Another pistol gleamed on the ground beside him. When I tucked behind a tree, and eased out my head just a little bit, I could easily spy his companion—a large man with the weathered look of a laborer, missing many teeth.

The two of them were a long stone's throw away, and even at this height the ceaseless rushing of the river below masked the sound of my steps as I hurried forward. Murray plied a ramrod, stuffing the black powder down the muzzle of his pistol.

I lost sight of them as I snaked through the bronze branches of the underbrush, twigs snatching at my clothes. Climbing forward on all fours, I powered ahead.

Pine scales clung to me, branches seizing my limbs as I hurried. The vegetation could not impede me. I was intent on nothing but sinking my knife into Murray, and I had to make haste, because when he got the pistol in his hands loaded and cocked, he would be dangerous again.

But at the same time I mocked my own fears. I had

spooked myself down there on the mountainside, convinced that I had been a heartbeat away from destruction. Surely I was foolish to be so afraid.

I strode quickly into the clearing, hastily rehearsed greetings running through my mind. I realized too late that I had misjudged Murray's readiness.

There was a lead pistol ball the size of a chestnut in his fingers, and he was just beginning to poke it down the barrel. But at the sight of me he interrupted the procedure. He reached for the other gun, on the pine needles beside him. He cocked it.

And leveled the firearm at me.

·◄[CHAPTER 42]►·

The toothless man took a step back, drawing a weapon from his belt.

Such burly men are without teeth not because of age or infirmity, I knew, but through fighting. His nose had been broken at some time in the past, and he had the scarred eyebrows of an experienced pugilist. He held a fierce, jagged weapon—a broken saber.

I was breathing hard, and took a long moment to break my silence.

Murray gave in to the impulse to speak, like a man of business interrupted by a footman. "What are *you* looking for?"

This was said with his old manner of abrasive authority, with emphasis on *you,* giving the impression that the only person with a rightful purpose was Murray himself. I gripped my knife hard, wondering if I could throw it and pierce his heart.

Murray squinted, to draw a bead with the big pistol in his hand—or so I assumed. But it's hard to keep a heavy weapon like that steady, and he lowered the flint-lock just slightly. Besides, as weary as I was from my climb, Murray was even more flushed and winded than I was—as though he had hauled a great weight onto this mountain ridge.

"I *know* you," he said at last.

He searched his memory.

"You're that fellow," he said with something like a wondering smile. He gave me a you-can't-fool-me wink. "From the carriage shop back home."

I said nothing.

People like Ezra and Samuel Murray were from established, genteel families. My station in life was well above that of a servant—as a skilled craftsman I was destined to occupy some middling rung in society. But while Ezra had taken the time to give me a smile and a bit of conversation, Murray had always glanced at me as he would a doorstop or a bootjack, an object.

Murray's smile faded just a little as he queried, "Aren't you?"

No one arrived in California, and traveled the foothills, looking the way he had on Walnut Street. My coat was flecked with long-dried mud, stained with horse sweat, and my boots were scuffed. I had not studied my suntanned, whiskery face in my tarnished mirror long enough to register more than a glimpse of a lean stranger.

I said, "I'm William Dwinelle."

Murray looked partly satisfied at this, but he needed further confirmation. "And you've come all this way?"

My intention until that moment had been to use my knife to gut Murray like a fish, and take great pleasure in the act.

Now, hearing his voice, and observing his manner, I changed my mind. I saw the way he looked at his big friend for approval, the gun trembling in his hand.

I couldn't, in all conscience, hurt him—not just yet.

"Where will you run?" I asked.

"Why should I run?" he asked. I knew, as well as he did, that the sons of rich families who violated even the most potent taboo could sail off to Tahiti, or even Paris, and live the grand life.

"Your family will wonder what became of you," I said—before I could think.

At once I silently cursed my bad judgment.

Uttering the word *family* had been a blunder. Family honor was plainly an obsession for Murray. Furthermore, I had inadvertently reminded him that I was a witness to the nature of his revenge. I would be able to tell all Philadelphia, and any legal proceeding, that Ezra had most likely not died in an evenhanded duel.

My newest, still developing plan was to keep him talking, win his confidence, and take his life before he could hurt me.

·◄[CHAPTER 43]►·

At the same time, in some half-mad way, I was glad to see Samuel Murray, happy to encounter someone from back home. I could almost will the present circumstances out of my mind.

Almost.

Murray was shaking his head with a nearly affectionate smile. He was sweating and breathing hard. "I'm sorry we don't have any refreshments to offer you, after your climb. I'm sure you'd like a glass of sherry right about now."

"Sure he would," said the scarred, toothless man.

It was as though a moss-clad boulder had spoken.

"So would any of us," said the big man, "or any kind of liquor."

A glance from Murray silenced him.

There was something forced and feverish about

Murray, despite his surface calm. "Billy," he began, then caught himself, and continued, "William, I do remember you pretty well. You're a capable hand."

I made no further remark.

"I recall you putting the rim on a wagon wheel, William," he continued, patronizingly, "with a certain flair."

I used to be proud of my ability, knowing that Murray and his kind were particularly incapable when it came to mending things.

"And you can repair a firearm, as I recall," Murray was continuing, in a self-controlled manner, his hand steady now.

He wanted me to say something at this point, but for the moment I would not give him the satisfaction.

"That's a useful skill," he added. His speech was that of a creature of money and leisure, habitually captured by his own confidence. For a moment I could see why a tough former boxer might prove loyal to such a man. Murray was unblushingly arrogant, and this made him a natural leader.

"I'll pay you five dollars a day, William," he went on, "to take up with me."

The pistol was easy in his hand now, pointed down toward the sandy ground. He moved the weapon a little as he spoke—an expensive-looking, rosewood-stocked gun—to give emphasis to his words.

"To travel around with me," he added. "And perform any little duty that might fall your way."

Some people can throw a knife hard enough to do harm, but it takes long practice. I had stropped my blade once or twice a week, and wiped it with gun oil from time to time, but doubted I could hurl the thing with any accuracy. I estimated the remaining distance between us. He was six long paces away from me—very long strides. I stayed right where I was for now, and did not make a sound.

"And, as proof of my confidence in you," Murray was saying with an air of breezy confidence, "I'll pay you a bonus, William. Forty dollars down."

His gaze flicked from my eyes to the knife in my hand, trying to read my intentions.

"Forty U.S. dollars," he continued. "Or the equivalent in gold dust."

He hesitated.

"Or," he said, "perhaps I can offer you more."

I rushed forward, angling the knife so the blade would drive upward—into his heart.

He brought up the pistol as my shadow was about to fall over him.

He pulled the trigger, and there was that characteristic split-second delay of such weapons, a flint spark and a sputtering whiff of smoke rising from the pan.

I never heard the shot.

·❧[CHAPTER 44]❧·

Time had passed, but I did not know how much.

I lay flat on my back. The sky stretched blue and empty overhead, and tall pines rose up on either side.

I believed that I was alive, but I was not sure. I breathed the enduring scent of gunpowder, an odor of sulfur and carbon. The sandy ground was hard, grit rasping against my cheek as I turned my head. I could not move my arms or legs for a long time. I lay there knitting together the time of day, and the events that had led up to my current condition.

I was in pain, and I was aware of a nagging, but still badly scattered sense of danger. It was afternoon, I reckoned, and I was alone. I had been unconscious for a good long while, perhaps hours.

After a very long time, I did manage to lift one hand and flex my fingers. I touched my coat buttons, trying to take reassurance from the fact that my hand answered my will. I groped up toward the charred wool of my jacket breast. I felt revulsion at the sensation of frizzled fiber, and the round, charred crater over my heart.

I could not move my left hand, my arm and my ribs paralyzed. But at once I contradicted this discovery, forcing myself into action as I struggled to my feet. I was exposed there, high above the campsite, and Murray could return at any moment.

I could move my arms after all. And I could walk, although shakily, first one step and then another. My ribs throbbed. My knife lay on the ground, and I groaned involuntarily as I snatched it from the sandy soil. I vomited, an agonizing spasm, but what my mouth emitted was the transformed relics of bacon and corn flour. There was no blood.

I cringed at the thought of probing a wound in my chest, but I made myself begin to do just that, feeling within my coat and gasping when I touched the warped, deformed metal there, what was left of my pewter flask of Dutch gin.

I extracted the wrecked container with effort, the dent left by the pistol ball clear and perfect, as though the round peen of a hammer had struck the metal. The bullet had flattened, and the flask dribbled what was left of the medicinal spirits. I was bruised and numb, but there was no wound.

Trees murmured and twigs sighed, the woodland breathing all around. Every tiny abrasion of branch against granite could be Murray and his companion, on their way back to finish me.

·≪{ CHAPTER 45 }≫·

I half climbed, half fell down the shrub-choked slope, all the way down into the camp. In my shaky condition, even this desolate ruin of a site was an improvement over the rocky woodland above.

By then the flies were thick around the two bodies, the sun brighter than ever. I half stumbled to the river, all the way out on the black sand of Spanish Bar, and splashed cold water on my arms and my face. I cupped some of the chilly water in my hand, and poured it over the fierce bruise on the white skin of my chest.

A sense of duty made me survey the delved and shoveled site, wondering which hole would be a suitable grave for my old friend and his fellow gold seeker. But then I reminded myself that it would be unwise and perhaps even illegal to bury them until civilized people had examined this scene. Somehow, there would have to be some sort of lawful proceeding—an inquest.

At the same time I felt naked. My Bowie knife now seemed puny. How little I could do to fight Murray off, I realized, if he returned. Something about the bloody mining tool made me cringe—I did not want to lay a hand on it. I found myself rummaging through the tent and found a hatchet, the iron edge grimy with pine sap.

As I let this tool fall, I heard a voice call out over the rush of the river. I turned to gaze at the shambles of the tent, telling myself I was certainly mistaken.

It rang out again—someone calling my name.

I stepped into daylight.

The source of the cry was a figure in gray: a miner's gray shirt, loose-fitting trousers, and a slouch hat. This individual called my name again, and bounded over the torn ground, carrying a shotgun.

I wondered where, exactly, I had dropped that perfectly good hatchet.

Well, then, I would die twice in one day, I thought, standing upright in the warm sunlight. I steeled myself for a charge of lead from both barrels.

The figure approached, her green eyes bright.

⊰[CHAPTER 46]⊱

I followed Florence on weak legs, my boots slipping from time to time as we made our way upriver.

I offered her a breathless, fragmented version of events as we hurried over the rocks and pine roots of the trail. She had much to tell me, too. Florence had snatched the gun off the ground before Jeremiah could stop her, and run to find me. She said that, as usual, she was much faster than any of her relations. "They're probably a mile or two off, even now," she said, "falling down in their hurry."

"I'm grateful to see you, Florence," I said.

"Watch your step here, William," she said. "Don't stumble on that broken log."

She leveled the shotgun every time we rounded a boulder on a bend in the river, lifting a hand to caution me.

We found them before long.

A rope had been stretched across the river by some enterprising miner in the recent past. Murray hung suspended from this makeshift crossing, clinging with white fists in the middle of the current. The rope was river-stained and slightly frayed where it dipped into the water. Murray's weight pulled it further, straining the span of cordage. His toothless companion had made it to the other side, and he cried out encouragement, his mouth working, his words soundless against the rush of the river.

Florence lifted the shotgun to her shoulder, and cocked both barrels.

You don't aim a gun like that so much as point it, estimating range with your eye. For a long moment I was frozen, sure that she was going to judge the gun capable of hitting the red-haired man.

"Don't waste the powder," I said, when I could move my lips.

When she didn't respond, I added, "He's too far away."

She said, "I know that."

It is the major drawback to scatterguns. Close in they can be deadly, but too far away they are only a source of noise.

She kept the double-barreled gun pressed to her shoulder, the very picture of menace. Murray waved beseechingly, calling out something in a tone of supplication. I could make out the words on his lips, *don't shoot,* and something else: explanation, promise—it was impossible to hear more than the drift of his voice. He patted his clothing meaningfully, indicating something secreted on his bulk.

She took long strides toward Murray, well out in the water now, the lapping current up round the shanks of her boots. She pressed the gun to her shoulder, and took the stance of a person well used to hunting.

I joined her, the cold river nearly to my boot tops. "It's still too far," I said quietly. I meant: Let him go.

I had seen enough violence.

Murray was wide-eyed, motioning with one hand while the hard current dragged him. The rope was pulled downriver by the weight of his body, and Florence kept both barrels steady, the muzzles of the barrels tracking him as he splashed.

Murray looked around to take in the sight of his imploring companion, then back at us with no further attempt to communicate. He measured the width of the river back and forth with his gaze, and took one more look at Florence, who was up to her waist now in the fast current.

She fired one barrel, a hard, punching sound over the roar of the rapids.

The shot went far wide, momentarily scarring the boiling current. But Murray, mouthing a curse, let go of the rope. He sank at once, down below the surface of the water. I expected to see his face again, breaking into the daylight, but there was no sign of him.

It was one thing to want to kill Murray, but quite another to stand there and watch him drown. I was in the icy water, scrambling over the boulders, wading out into the current. I fought the pull of the current, but as I struggled for better footing, my legs were swept out from under me. I swam hard, my ribs aching, right for the place where I expected Murray to reappear.

But he did not surface again. Something forced him down to the bottom of the river, and through the streaks of current I could see him struggling, his arms reaching, flailing in the depths.

···⊰[CHAPTER 47]⊱···

My own garments, my belt and my boots, were dragging me down. I fought hard against my own sodden weight, and against the cold current, until I reached Murray. His arms were drifting now, strengthlessly, but one of his limp hands wafted out toward me, and I clung to it.

I could not pull him up. The lingering life in him wrenched his hand from mine, and when I found him once more he was a man of stone, a figure I could not lift. I struggled to the sunlight, drank in deep, sweet drafts of air, and then I was underwater again, groping, searching.

This time I folded him over my shoulder and half swam, half trudged along the river bottom, my feet slipping, the breath burning in my lungs. By the time I saw clear daylight and breathed oxygen, Florence was out in the river again, clinging to the rope, reaching out for me.

She seized me as I struggled to drag Murray. I was gasping, the cold numbing me, Murray's bulk impossibly heavy. I was barely able to cling to him against the force of the river, and I wrestled with the slowly rolling form until I heard welcome voices, Johnny and bearded Timothy wading out into the rapids, calling to me, lending me their helping hands.

We dragged Murray out of the water, and higher, all the way up to the torn and shoveled mining claim, and stretched him out there in the brilliant sunlight.

His mouth was agape and his eyes fixed, the water puddling wide around his body. I tugged my knife from its sheath, and used the blade to cut open the source of Murray's unnatural weight, his bulging pockets.

For an instant it looked like blood, the spilling, richly flowing stuff pouring from the gashes in his clothing.

It was gold.

PART THREE
THE RIVER

·⋅{ CHAPTER 48 }⋅·

"There's another bear in the supply shed," reported Johnny.

"Talk to it, Johnny. Tell it to go away," I said, too busy shoveling wet gravel into the mining cradle to bother with an interruption.

Spanish Bar had turned out to be a veritable thoroughfare for every drowsy, half-starved bear in the Sierra foothills. The incessant mining activity aroused them from hibernation. Word was that a miner from Georgia had been found clawed to death near Iowa Hill.

"It won't come out," replied Johnny.

He had just returned from the Barrymore camp with a sack of coffee and some plug tobacco, and I had left our supply shed unattended in his absence.

Grizzly bears, especially she-bears with cubs, could

be a menace, but the common brown bears were harmless, if powerful, vagrants, breaking their hibernation with occasional raids on poorly secured larders. We had not seen a grizzly here in the foothills, but the brown bruins had helped themselves to our bacon and our cornmeal, breaking into the shed as fast as I could repair it.

I made my way across the dug-up claim, hoping a word from me would discourage our most recent guest.

I was sorry Florence was not here. She was living at Dutch Bar, under the watchful eyes of her family. She would have known what to do with a bear, or any other sort of intruder.

It was a cold morning in the winter of 1850. Five weeks had passed since the deaths of Ezra and the others. Cholera and rising river waters were devastating Sacramento City. I didn't go down there to observe the disaster at first hand, occupied as I was helping the Barrymores working the Nevin-Follette claim. The family had bought the claim at an auction at Welsh Flat, the proceeds to go to the kin of the two gentlemen back in Philadelphia, along with the tidy fortune we had found on Murray's body.

I liked the Barrymores. They paid me a fair share of the gold flakes I dug out of the sodden ground, but my future was in repairing the iron tools breaking and losing their edge all over the Sierra foothills. Captain Deerborn had a new shipment arriving any day from Baltimore. He could use a younger partner, he had said, who could hawk ironware from Shirt Tail Canyon to Grass Valley and back, and I agreed with him that the sale and repair of such items was the smartest way to put color in my strongbox.

Captain Deerborn had held an inquest at Welsh Flat the week before Christmas. I testified at the outdoor legal proceeding, which the captain himself—resplendent in newly polished spurs—had presided over as acting coroner. I put my hand on the Bible and told what I had seen.

The jury of Forty-niners, including Aaron Sweetland and Jeremiah Barrymore, delivered a verdict of homicide, and charged the late Samuel Van Buren Murray of Philadelphia with the crime. The unknown toothless pugilist was listed as an accessory and was still at large. Most observers were of the opinion that his luckless remains would be found during the spring thaw, wolf-gnawed in one of the mountain passes.

I had used my best penmanship in describing Ezra's good fortune and untimely death to Elizabeth, but I kept tossing the half-completed letters into the campfire. I was running out of blank pages in Ezra's journal, and I accepted the fact that any letter writing would have to wait. I would send a good portion of my own earnings back to Elizabeth, to help Ezra's child get a start in life, but the young woman I had known in Philadelphia was already changing from a living presence to someone I had trouble remembering.

Now I was standing outside our lean-to, watching

as the makeshift structure swayed, the creature inside just visible through the slats in the wooden walls.

I struck the side of the shed with my shovel, and the animal responded by leaning nearly all his weight on the plank wall, forcing the square-headed nails to loosen with a chorus of squeaks.

"He's very stubborn," said Johnny, already prepared to forgive my failure.

Not wanting to disappoint Johnny, I struck the shed again. The shovel blade made a sour clang against the planks.

The bear gave a windy sigh, and made its way out of the structure, but as it departed it caught a glimpse of me.

It must have seen a youthful gold miner going pale—two of us, standing there without a hope in the world.

Good luck had failed us.

Our visitor was a grizzly.

··❦ CHAPTER 49 ❦··

The beast's distinctive, upturned *Ursus horribilis* snout was thickly glazed with brown sugar. The unexpected sight of such a potentially threatening bear made me grow very quiet, the shovel a feeble potential weapon in my grasp. The bear turned, huge, its breath steaming in the morning air, observing me once more with its tiny black eyes.

"If we don't do anything unexpected," said Johnny, keeping his voice from shaking too much, "it should move off."

"I've heard that they will," I agreed.

Although I kept my composure, I was terrified. An ax leaned against the woodpile, the nearest thing to a lethal weapon in the camp. Our hatchet was long since beyond repair. The mining tools stacked over by the campfire were the sort of implements that would annoy a bear before they drew blood. I would never have considered using my knife against such a great beast.

The bear shuffled upslope, slowly, taking its own good time.

"Don't yell at it," I cautioned.

"I was standing here perfectly quietly," Johnny answered.

He was right. I gave him a nod of apology.

"Unless it rushes us," added Johnny. "Then I'll start yelling."

The bear made imperial progress, stopping to bite the head off a winter-blanched weed among the graves we had dug for Ezra and the others.

The Barrymores had helped make the resting places of the two gentlemen as handsome as possible, bordered with pretty rose-veined quartz. There were worse places on earth to be buried, no doubt. Nevertheless I hoped that when I lay down my bones, it might be in a town somewhere, near carriages and the passing footsteps of neighbors.

The grizzly chose a route between two pines, and with surprising ease and swiftness he vanished.

I waited for a long time.

A gray-and-red woodpecker alighted on a tree stump.

When I was certain that the bear was well away from the camp, I accepted the printed circular Johnny was holding out to me. I had to wonder what opera singer or tragedian had made it as far as Welsh Flat, the farthest east any performer could comfortably travel.

"Great Ladies of Shakespeare," proclaimed the theatrical bill. "Performed by Sarah Encard, direct from London and Paris. With Love Scenes of the Bard, reenacted by Constance Castleman and Benjamin DuLac."

I gave a delighted start.

DuLac. Ben had grown shameless. But this was wonderful news.

"Everyone's excited about the stage play," said Johnny, "all up and down the river."

"They ought to be," I said. My heart was beating hard, and I remembered that I had once lived far away from this muddy hole beside a river, in a city with tall, shady sycamores.

It had been difficult to court Florence, but I was capable of a sort of friendly stubbornness. I had not mustered the power of speech that would allow me to ask her to marry me, but I was well on my way. We sometimes met beside the river, after dark.

"Johnny," I said, "I wonder if there's a boot brush in Ezra's trunk."

"A fine ivory-handled one," said Johnny.

Johnny was smart and strong, for his size, and capable in every way. But sometimes he had lapses in his understanding.

"Why do you need a boot brush?" he was asking, as

though none of us were soiled through to the skin and in need of every sort of cleaning implement ever manufactured.

I was too thrilled to stand there any longer, but ran to get ready.

Tonight I was taking Florence to the theater.

D.